The Official Guide to the Right Toys

DR. HELEN BOEHM

Over 200 brand name toys sure to bring joy, foster skills and stimulate children of every age and stage of development.

First published by AuthorHouse 02/24/05

ISBN: 1-4208-2958-0 (Paperback)

This book is printed on acid free paper.

Contents:

PART 4: TOYS FOR SCHOOL-AGED CHILDREN

Foreword:

Play has long been considered the basic curriculum of early childhood, with toys and games the primary subjects. Watch young children at play – their version of "work" – and you will observe youngsters learning about the world around them, experimenting with how things work and rehearsing the roles of adulthood. Play affords an important vehicle for learning and toys are the necessary tools.

Parents and grandparents already know the vital role that toys play in the development of a child's skills and abilities. But, selecting the "right" age-appropriate playthings is an awesome task and a huge responsibility. With thousands of new toys hitting the market each year, selecting the right toys that fit the needs of the children in your life can be a challenging and overwhelming task.

Enter Dr. Helen Boehm, who has thankfully taken much of the guesswork out of the process and provided us with a flexible prescription for selecting the "right" toy for the "right" age and ability. Parents and grandparents now have a simple-to-use roadmap for making toy decisions based on solid child development criteria. Choosing toys that will help children master important developmental milestones and have fun in the process has just become a whole lot easier!

What follows is a guide to selecting toys from a developmental and educational perspective. The reader is going to learn how baby's first toys introduce exploration and discovery as well as enhance her sensory awareness, how a toddler's relentless curiosity teaches her about consequences and how active preschoolers can use pretend play to reinforce nurturing skills and empathy.

Most importantly, parents and grandparents will use the information garnered from these pages to interact with their children in the way they know best. Through play, they will enter the magical world of childhood and share in this significant time of learning and loving.

Maria Weiskott

Editor In Chief
Playthings Magazine

Introduction:

In the same way that our own work may be frustrating without the right tools, our children's play may be less challenging – and not as much fun – without the right toys. Play is the "job description" of childhood, and a more educational and rewarding task cannot be found. For, it is during play that children develop important skills and spend time rehearsing the roles of adulthood.

The "right" and most appropriate toys are those that challenge children's interests and are closely linked to their skills and abilities. Sounds simple, but selecting the "right" toys is anything but child's play!

Educators and psychologists guide research on child development and investigate how youngsters learn. But, parents have long known what these studies seem to confirm; that children learn spontaneously, continuously and naturally during play.

Watching children at play demonstrates that learning is a developmental process. Whether in the crib or in the classroom, play is a prerequisite to many future problem-solving abilities and abstract thinking aptitudes. As children move through ages and stages, their playthings and interactions become more complex. Therefore, at six months or six years of age, children's days are still well spent, hard at work - at play.

Ask the savviest shopper -- a mother on a budget – and she will concede that finding toys to fit her child's unique needs and interests is an awesome challenge. I therefore wrote this book to share some useful parenting insights about toys and to shed light on the role of play in the learning process. My purpose was to provide you, the reader, with specific suggestions regarding the best toys currently on the market that meet the distinctive requirements of children at different developmental stages.

Like millions of other parents, I have walked the aisles of toy stores in search of the "right" toys. Most of these shopping trips left me overwhelmed by the endless array of choices available. And, although the selection of good toys was enormous, little information was available to guide me through the maze of *which* products were the "right" toys for my individual child.

In arranging this book for ease of use, I have grouped recommendations by "age-appropriateness" and special interest areas. Age classifications based on developmental milestones -- or the ages at which most children accomplish certain tasks or demonstrate specific behaviors -- are useful because they provide general reference points and help to predict future performance. Although generalizations about large groups of children at certain ages can be helpful in selecting toys - they do *not* explain variations between individual children, nor should serve as rigid markers for evaluating any child.

No two youngsters develop at quite the same rate or will use a toy in precisely the same way. Children have particular play styles and strategies, which are as unique as the youngsters themselves. Since toys will change and grow along with kids, the categories in this book should serve as guideposts - not rules - for selecting appropriate toys.

The "right" toys included in this book are representative of many other excellent products of similar quality. Member companies of the Toy Industry Association (TIA), the international toy trade group, were invited to submit products for review and evaluation. Playthings selected for inclusion in this book had to meet the safety standards prescribed by the TIA as well as those regulations imposed by the United States Consumer Product Safety Commission (CPSC). But, perhaps most importantly, the toys included in this book passed the very stringent criteria and high standards of the most discerning judges of all -- children found them fun to play with!

Which skills are reinforced by which toys?

Look for the **"RIGHT*RATING"*** icons that appear directly below each photograph in this book. The **"RIGHT*RATING"*** is a tool to help you quickly identify the underlying play value of a specific toy. Discover the three major "learning benefits" of each product to determine which toy will best meet *your* child's *individual* needs. **"RIGHT*RATING"*** icons will guide you in selecting playthings that are appropriate for your child's unique learning style and strengths.

 Cognitive (thinking and problem-solving skills)

 Visual Discrimination (observing and seeing)

 Visual/Motor Skills (eye-hand coordination)

 Auditory Discrimination (listening)

 Tactile (touching and physical connection)

 Creativity (imagination and artistic skills)

 Large Motor (coordination, running and climbing)

 Small Motor (fine coordination and finger dexterity)

 Instructional (facts and pre-academic learning)

 Socialization (cooperative play with empathy)

 Independence (individuality and self-confidence)

PART 1: TOYS FOR INFANTS

TOYS FOR THE FIRST 6 MONTHS

TOYS FOR THE 6-12 MONTH -OLD

TOYS FOR THE 12-18 MONTH -OLD

Chapter 1: Toys for the First 6 Months of Life

The birth of a baby is a magnificent event – and the excitement has just begun! The newborn enters the world with the capacity to learn and the blueprint for future intellectual, physical and social development. The right toys - from the very start - can be a springboard for discovery and stimulation. Toys, under the magical direction of a baby at play, become transformed into tools for exploring and understanding the world.

In the recent past, gifts for new babies were primarily soft goods like blankets and layette clothing. Toys were rarely considered appropriate presents for newborns, in part because there were few toys on the market created specifically for infants and also because there was widespread belief that new babies really didn't "do" much.

We now know, however, that from the first moments of life, the newborn actively responds to - and directs - her environment. The right playthings can challenge that responsive awareness. Numerous toys have been developed to enhance the youngest infant's ability to explore and interact with the world and reinforce early learning. These items arouse baby's attention and foster the growth of sensory skills.

New babies should be provided with visual, auditory and tactile opportunities to enhance discovery and learning. Not only will these toys enrich a baby's play, they also facilitate important cognitive and physical development. During the first six months, playthings provide a meaningful link between the baby and her environment and contribute significantly to the early learning process. For the developing infant, awareness and active exploration best occurs in an atmosphere of fun and joyful play.

Through looking, listening, feeling and mouthing babies investigate, discover and learn. As early as the first weeks of life, newborns demonstrate an interest in following lights as well as black and red patterns. An infant's primary means of investigation is through her mouth until she develops the strength necessary to lift and turn her head to reveal new views and angles on the world. Over the next few months, the ability to reach, grasp and hold objects will present increased opportunities to gain important competencies. As baby matures, her eyes and hands become a critical team for gathering and processing information.

The crib setting should reflect the newborn's emerging interests and stimulate curiosity in the larger environment. It should contain toys that heighten awareness of baby's surroundings, and also of herself. These playthings should motivate the exploration of objects, be engaging to play with and fun. Soft, cuddly toys can also assist in maintaining a sense of calm, warmth and security. But, most importantly, infants need the attention and affection of parents and caregivers as well as a safe and loving environment. Some of the right toys for stimulating growth and development during the first six months of life are:

Learning Patterns Changing Sensations Mobile
(Fisher-Price

A crib mobile may be attractive from an adult point of view - looking down from above the crib. But, when the mobile is tilted toward baby looking *up* and adjusted directly to her range of visibility, it truly challenges her developing senses. Baby is excited as she anticipates movement and is reinforced by the patterns and animal shapes that pass through her field of vision. The movement of objects suspended in front of her face bring the dancing critters into clear view. This mobile provides continuing opportunities to focus attention on interesting objects and investigate movement and light from the important visual perspective of the developing infant.

My Very Soft Baby
(Playskool)

During the earliest months of life, the infant may develop an attachment to a particular soft doll. This special toy can act as an anchor when there is confusion in her environment and can engage her sustained interest in something outside of herself. Baby's first doll should be soft and durable and have no sewn-on features that can become undone or loosened. Although the infant may not be able to carry her doll for several months, she can swat and pat her special friend. This baby doll makes a giggle sound and is soft bodied for nurturing and cuddling. And, it can be mouthed, dampened and washed to keep both the doll and the baby clean and healthy.

5

Lamb Comfy Cozy
(GUND)

Perhaps baby's very first toy, this silky lamb blanket is actually part security blanket and part stuffed animal. Baby can be swaddled in the blanket while playing with the face and paws of the soft, plush lamb doll. As a play mat, crib or carriage blanket, baby will be stimulated and entertained while playing within inches of her field of vision. This secure "environment" brings the infant into a three-dimensional play setting where she can touch and explore a soft, stuffed animal while still safely wrapped in a cozy, baby blanket.

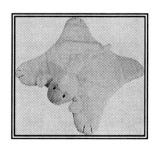

Kick Start Gym
(Playskool)

Physical activity begins during the first minutes of life. During a baby's earliest weeks, swatting, kicking and reaching movements become increasingly purposeful. These kicking motions stimulate physical development and attention by encouraging baby to use her physicality and natural thrusting and reaching instincts to activate music and sounds. Brightly colored shapes and hanging beads respond to her reaching movements. This stimulating "kicking gymnasium" reinforces baby's large-motor and muscular development as well as her sensory awareness. Establishing cause and effect relationships and having an impact upon her environment are the beginnings of independent play and reinforce repeated activity and interaction.

6

Music in Motion Developmental Mobile
(Sassy)

During the first few weeks of life, baby's range of vision only extends 10 to 12 inches from her face. However, when interesting items move across this range, she will immediately focus on, and follow, the objects in motion. Mobiles can act as a foundation for the development of visual tracking skills. And, when music is added to the movement, the crib becomes a stimulating multi-sensory environment. This innovative mobile has movement and sound elements that can be activated by remote control, so its music and movement can be turned on and off without ever waking a sleeping baby.

The Babbler
(Neurosmith)

This washable and very soft toy provides baby with stimulating auditory experiences and opportunities to distinguish among an array of sounds. While encouraging attention and listening skills, this interactive product lays the groundwork for later language learning. Through early exposure to auditory stimuli and verbal cues, concentration and vocalization abilities are strengthened and a foundation for successful language learning is established. Sounds - including "scrunching", "rattling" and "honking" - become the backdrop for recorded voices that actually "babble" foreign language sounds in Spanish, French and Japanese! Sensory stimulation such as blinking lights reinforces the recorded sounds.

Sounding Shapes
(BRIO)

As the new baby explores her first toys, she gathers information about the world around her. While grasping and holding this toy, she is stimulated by the colors, shapes, sounds and the power to make things appear and disappear. Baby discovers that she can affect the ladybug's "crinkling"; bee's "buzzing" and mouse's "squeaking" as she connects that one event will cause the other to follow. As the infant investigates the source of each sound and becomes aware of her ability to make things happen, her attention is sharpened and her eye-hand coordination is also reinforced.

Baby Beethoven Musical Ring Teether
(Baby Einstein)

Important future skills, such as writing, drawing and using hand tools, evolve from the mastery of grasping and holding. Hand-held rattle activity toys encourage hand dexterity and eye-hand coordination as well as visual-motor development. As a simple learning devise, holding and moving the rattle will motivate interaction as the soft plastic surface encourages exploration by mouth and hands. While baby shakes this toy, she begins to connect her actions with musical sounds that set the stage for cause and effect learning. This rattle plays Beethoven's "Fifth Symphony" as baby tracks its sounds and movement.

Natural Bell Rattle
(Maple Landmark)

Even the slightest movement of this rattle emits the soothing timber of a small ringing bell. The newborn can localize a sound within minutes of birth and focus her interest in the direction of the sound. A simple rattle's movement and ringing engages baby and motivates her interaction and inspection. This traditional wooden rattle can be easily held and mouthed for exploration. It will encourage the infant's responses that begin with the turning of her head toward the direction of the sound and is followed by swatting, reaching and grasping at the item responsible for the sound.

Learning Patterns Jungle Pal Music Mirror
(Fisher-Price)

Baby's discovery of her own image, separate from that of her mother, is a developmental milestone. A crib mirror promotes self-awareness and begins the process of building self-esteem. Baby will stare at her own image in the mirror, although she won't actually recognize herself, just yet. In addition to staring at this angled mirror, she will use the dangling toys attached to the mirror as props for reaching and clutching. At about 3 months, as she begins to raise her head for an extended period, this product can be positioned in front of her so she can look at herself from a brand new vantage point.

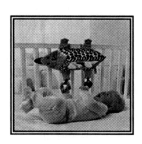

Inchworm Lamaze
(Learning Curve)

This soft crib toy combines the elements of surprise, visual stimulation and sound to encourage baby to respond and react to her environment. High contrast black and white graphics attract attention to a medley of crinkle and squeaking noises. And, when the baby rolls over next to the inchworm, there is a tape measure to keep track of her early growth. This toy invites investigation and offers numerous visual, auditory and tactile discoveries. Placed next to baby in the crib, it can be touched and cuddled. Tied to the crib rails, it facilitates inspection, swinging and swatting.

Discover and Play Activity Gym
(Baby Einstein)

This flexible play center is designed to stimulate sensory integration and support physical and perceptual coordination. With motion, music, and high-contrast patterns dangling overhead, this gym frame extends the infant's interest into the world and provides an incentive to exercise muscles, visual-tracking skills and imagination. The colorful hanging objects encourage baby to bat and swipe with her arms and further extend her range of motion. Among the classical melodies played are Bach's "Goldberg Variations" and the "Brandenburg Concerto". A soft book, ring rattle and flash card holder are also included.

Early Years Crib Mirror
(International Playthings)

Black and white high-contrast graphics attract baby's attention to this distortion-free crib mirror. As baby watches her own reflection and mimics her own moves, she begins to establish a sense of separate self and a recognition of her ability to change the reflections of light that she sees. As the infant begins to play and become self-aware, she will experience visual cause and effect relationships. Since baby is almost immediately aware of light and patterns, a crib mirror can encourage socialization, vocalization and motor activity.

Light 'N Sound Clown
(*Chicco*)

A first "multi-sensory" toy, this easy-to-grasp rattle provides the infant with a real interactive experience. Flashing lights, colorful rattling balls and music are activated by baby as she holds and shakes this innovative rattle. A stimulating and responsive toy, noise and light attract baby's attention and provide her with concrete auditory cues. Exploring the cause and effect relationship that her movement has inspired will be a significant part of her early learning. Predicting outcomes will focus her attention on the impact of her actions. As she discovers these predictable pleasant effects, such as sounds and lights, she will increase the behaviors that inspired them.

11

II

Chapter 2: Toys for 6- to 12 Month-Olds

The second half of baby's first year is filled with great leaps in physical and cognitive abilities. Unbounded curiosity, exploration and activity characterize this period. The excitement of creeping and crawling allow independent investigations to extend baby's world far beyond the crib or playpen. And the ability to control arms, legs and hands significantly widens her learning horizons.

At six months, newly developed muscular strength and coordination enables baby to experience the world from brand new positions – those of sitting and standing – and view, manipulate and drop objects from this exciting new perspective.

During this developmental period, sounds are transformed into words and used in a purposeful way. The beginning use of language is reinforced by the infant's awareness that words like "mama", "hot" and "hat" are actually labels used to communicate, and that words represent the names or functions of people, places, concepts and objects. Also during these months, the baby makes tremendous strides in her social and emotional development. She now shows her separateness from mother and readily demonstrates fear, surprise, anger and happiness.

As the child approaches her first birthday, she is desperate to understand how things work. These efforts are fueled by increased fine motor ability and refined physical agility. As she investigates and manipulates objects with her hands and mouth, she begins to explore and differentiate their characteristics. In doing so, babies of this age have the continuing opportunity to compare and contrast what they touch, taste and smell and begin to sort and classify information.

Through play, baby learns about herself, what she can and cannot do and how she can influence her environment. She is becoming an assertive individual, aware of her ability to impact the world. By internalizing the connection between what she does and the response that occurs, she becomes empowered to push a button, turn a dial or press a lever. Maturing motor skills such as dexterity and grasp enable play to become an opportunity to explore cause and effect relationships. And, when learning that actions have consequences, the infant develops a cognitive strategy for information processing and problem solving. The following toys are recommended for babies between six and twelve months of age and foster play experiences that assist learning and growth:

Talk and Flash Camera
(The First Years)

As baby approaches her first birthday, her dexterity and small motor skills increase, as does her ability to observe and imitate behavior. Fantasy play with a child-sized version of something she sees used often helps her to role-play with confidence. This soft play camera has mirrors for lenses that inspire fun and self-awareness. As the toy is handled, it makes actual camera sounds and even has a "flash" that lights up. The camera lens clicks so baby can pretend she is using a real camera. And, there are "crinkle" and "rattle" sounds for additional crib play.

Hello Bee... Hello Me
(Sassy)

Early exposure to books is the basis for a lifelong interest in reading. Experience handling books helps baby feel comfortable with the written word and establishes positive attitudes toward learning and reading. This first book builds on children's fascination with faces and promotes attention, concentration and visual-tracking skills. Simple animal pictures and a wonderful baby mirror encourage communication and introduce baby to the warm experience of reading and cuddling with parents. A smile at the bee - or the baby in the mirror - establishes a firm and early connection between fun, discovery, learning and a love of reading.

Stacking Cups
(Battat)

Hands-on play with an assortment of various sized Stacking Cups introduces baby to sorting by size and patterns. Investigating how things work and fit together as well as the nesting and building relationships of these cups, engages baby's interest and curiosity. Stacking by size or just putting one cup on top of another strengthens coordination. There is not just one "correct placement" for using various cups for discovery and experimentation, and all ways enhance imagination and creativity. Decorated with numbered pictures of objects, problem-solving skills are developed as baby figures out how to stack, balance and knock down small towers.

My First 1-2-3 Puppets Book
(Folkmanis)

Baby's first books should combine soft activity pages for play with the surprise and ritual of page turning. Visually interesting and easy to manipulate materials, like the finger puppets and motor activities found in this book, reinforce the fun of interacting with books as the underpinning to future reading. Three-dimensional play materials enhance learning and object, letter and number recognition. This fabric - constructed book exposes baby to numbers 1-10 and to counting concepts using glove and finger puppetry.

Pop-Up Talking Farm
(Chicco)

Investigation and discovery lead to stimulating learning experiences. Babies manipulate toys because they want to understand what playthings do as well as how they work. This activity toy stimulates curiosity and teaches visual and auditory association. Farm animals, each with their own special barnyard sound, help baby to learn the relationship between animals and the sounds they make. Doors and windows of this activity center barn open and close to provide opportunities for fantasy play and interaction.

 S Motor
 Auditory
 Cognitive

Leapstart Learning Table
(LeapFrog)

This interactive, musical activity table provides a stimulating environment for exploration and development. There are numerous activities and effects to explore. Early concept formation involving counting, shapes and color recognition keep baby engaged and entertained. Spinning, pulling, pushing, sliding and rolling are important manipulative skills which baby can practice while using this educational desktop. During play, realistic sound effects and familiar melodies are used to increase and enhance learning activities.

 Cognitive
 Skills
 Auditory

17

My First Tools
(GUND)

Babies spend more time sleeping or lying in their cribs than just about anywhere else. Therefore, the crib is baby's classroom and it should be a stimulating and exciting learning environment. This soft toolbox filled with small, stuffed "tool-shaped" playthings provides visual stimulation and high contrast sound effects. A hammer that "rattles", screwdriver that "crinkles" and wrench that "squeaks" offer many visual, auditory and tactile discoveries. At first, baby will grasp the tools with her entire hand. Later, she will refine her exploration to bring together her thumb and fingers in opposition as she inspects and mouths the shapes and textures.

Stack and Nest Aquarium
(Manhattan Toy)

Between 6 and 12 months, baby's developing visual and motor skills allow her to fit and pile large multi-textured materials. Each of the four jumbo-sized cups in this soft toy contains its own surprise: a mirror, fish puppet, "swimming" fish or rattle. Stacking and nesting objects help baby sharpen her perceptual and concentration abilities and small motor planning. Through repeated play with this toy, baby discovers how various items interact and the comparative concepts of size and shape and larger than and smaller than. During this time of rapid physical and intellectual development, problem-solving, abstract thinking and learning strategies are also reinforced.

Poundin' Bedbugs
(Playskool)

This toy assists in the development of perceptual and small motor skills. Cause and effect relationships are fortified as colorful pegs pop up and down in response to baby's pounding and banging. This bench is a variation of the classic wooden cobbler's bench adapted in size, weight and material and geared to the skill level of children under a year of age. Since baby's strength and coordination are still developing, plastic "bugs" are easily forced down or sprung up to greet pounding motions. And, as eye-hand coordination, visual accuracy and grasping skills improve, baby will experience success and visible reinforcement from play that models "work."

. Ocean Wonders Aquarium
(Fisher-Price)

As baby begins to sit independently, she no longer needs her arms for balance. Her hands are free to inspect, grasp, manipulate, push and pull objects while she sits in her crib. Toys securely mounted on the side of the crib can motivate the growing infant to participate in a variety of small motor activities and build dexterity and eye-hand coordination. This toy contains activities for building appropriate skills by exposing youngsters to levers and roller balls. During less active periods, this flexible toy can help a child by providing transitions to napping with its calming music and relaxing water sounds.

Air-Tivity Whirl Around
(Playskool)

Simple dexterity skills, such as grasping and pressing, are developed during baby's exploration of this stimulating hand held rattle. This colorful toy is easily activated by the pressure of an infant's hand and provides a stimulating visual tracking experience. As baby presses a large textured button, bright beads are activated to float through clear passageways and capture her attention. She is reinforced for her manipulation and begins to focus on the movement of the colorful balls through the clear channels. This toy helps develop holding and gripping skills, and builds hand strength and hand-to-hand movement.

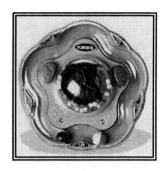

Twist, Rock & Roll
(VTech)

Educational playthings should respond to children around the activities that they do naturally – like play. This rolling drum interacts with baby by playing melodies in response to her movements and encouraging her to continue creating sound effects by moving and crawling. Music and sound inspire and reinforce movement while allowing the baby to develop a range of cognitive and motor abilities. A letter and number recognition mode on the drum provides skill-based activities that promote intellectual and social development. As the child grows she can use this product in increasingly challenging ways.

Build-a-Clown
(North American Bear Co.)

Developmentally appropriate stacking and nesting toys help baby gain perceptual abilities and complete small motor tasks. This brightly colored clown has a "noisy-nose" and a body comprised of plush rings. As baby coordinates her hand movements with her visual tracking, she experiences success and gains confidence. This toy facilitates holding and gripping and helps to develop dexterity. As baby plays, eye-hand coordination is rehearsed and refined. Children between six and twelve months can now inspect toys and play from a new, seated perspective.

Lamaze Clutch Cube
(Learning Curve)

As baby approaches her first birthday, the exploration and investigation of interesting objects becomes an important aspect of her day and play. This colorful cube puts the control right in the palm of baby's hand. The bright colors and contrasting patterns stimulate visual attention and an interior jingle sharpens acuity and auditory awareness. Each handle that baby grabs offers a different shape, texture and color. As baby responds to both sound and touch, she is learning and being entertained. A practical soft crib toy, this cube is safe for use in either a prone or sitting position, and will cushion, not obstruct, any falls.

Stack and Discovery Rings
(VTech)

Important eye hand coordination and visual-discrimination skills are reinforced during play with this interactive stacking tower. Fit and drop relationships, as well as stacking skills are encouraged. In addition, problem solving abilities are strengthened as the baby grasps, stacks, and sequences colorful rings and is rewarded with flashing lights and silly sounds. Each stacking arm of this 4-pronged tower plays a different melody so baby can repeat the stacking action again and again. These accumulating and combining behaviors are the groundwork for later construction activities and more complex combinations of materials, weights and measures.

Chapter 3: Toys for 12-to 18-Month-Olds

Baby's first birthday and first steps, milestones that often occur simultaneously, signal a readiness for new challenges in play. The toddler now directs her seemingly limitless energy toward investigating and interacting with the world from an upright and mobile position. Important attitudes toward active participation and interaction with the environment are developed through early play experiences and remain a prominent physical theme throughout life.

While investigating and manipulating objects, baby acquires and practices new skills while she comes to understand the impact of her actions. By internalizing the connection between what she does and what happens to her, she begins to anticipate outcomes and gain self-control. The one-year-old embraces every possible opportunity to inspect, carry, push, drop, hug, take apart objects and put them back together. During these explorations, physical activity abounds and baby's movement – between naps - seems practically continuous.

Language acquisition is rapid in the months that follow a youngster's first birthday. At this age, the development of speech is based primarily on the observation and imitation of others. Play provides an excellent opportunity to listen to and mimic sounds, songs and words.

While relating to her toys, the young toddler gathers information through a variety of concrete, hands-on experiences. Gaining this data through "doing" rather than observing is a valuable and effective process. Studies confirm that concepts are more readily understood and more accurately remembered when information is experienced – rather than simply received. Toys should be selected to provide this type of educational experience as well as physical challenges and language-rich opportunities.

Often, play with two or more young toddlers occurs in close proximity but is usually independent and without interaction. However, even playing near other children and simply observing siblings and peers during parallel play can significantly enrich the life of a one-year-old. As children discover their connection to each other and the larger environment, toys that encourage socialization will promote interaction, language attainment and social skills. Toys selected to meet the physical, cognitive and social-emotional challenges of the one and a half-year-old include:

Together Time
(LeapFrog)

Designed to nurture and stimulate parent-child communication, numerous developmental activities are integrated into this interactive system. While playing with this product, the child is exposed to age-appropriate learning concepts while enhancing her foundation for reading, language, math and music. The "Storytime" experience includes a Leap Pad, software and books and provides varied presentations and a large range of information. Learning takes place at several distinct levels and prepares children for problem solving, letter and word recognition and opportunities to use their imagination and creativity. In addition, parent-child bonding is reinforced during this shared learning endeavor and positive socialization activity.

Humpty Dumpty
(Eden)

As baby pulls along this clicking and clacking toy, she announces to the world that she is a toddler, extremely mobile and able to move along quickly on her own. This spurt of confidence further motivates her large motor activity and sharpens her motor planning and balance. As she moves in a purposeful and coordinated way, Humpty Dumpty follows, reinforcing her ability to impact and control the world, create noise and make things happen. And, as she guides the toy, she can begin to role-play the nurturing, "come-along" parent and guide.

Puzzibilities Sounds on the Farm
(Small World)

First puzzles with large knobs and limited pieces encourage success and build confidence. The toddler's memory, eye-hand coordination and hand and finger grasp are all enhanced as she holds small knobs and fits large wooden pieces into their proper places. Trial and error strategies are reinforced as the familiar pictures of farm animals also produce animal sounds. The child feels capable and proud as she finishes her task and is rewarded by farm sounds as well as a picture that she has completed, independently. Bright, contrasting pictures capture the child's interest and stimulate the visual differentiation of pieces, so the energetic toddler can sit, focus, listen and solve this puzzle quickly and easily.

Geometric Shapes Jumbo Knob Puzzle
(Lights, Camera, Interaction)

This puzzle is designed to teach colors and shapes while reinforcing coordination, perceptual motor and problem solving skills. It challenges the toddler with large, easy-to-grab knobs that help her move, cover and remove each piece while matching it to the color illustration found underneath. A red circle and octagon, yellow rectangle and pentagon, blue oval and triangle, and green diamond and square can be removed and then placed back in their correct spaces in a sequence that is simple and geared for success. Independent play experiences with puzzles such as this encourage skill development, attention building and the prediction of consequences.

Puppy Pull Toy
(BRIO)

Pull toys reinforce motor planning, direction, balance and large motor coordination. Movement of this toy enhances the child's visual and motor development as she pulls the toy while walking forward and continually checks back to see its performance and constant feedback. This toy happily follows its owner, providing security for always being there and amusement as it twists its head, wags its tail and moves its ears. Since the slightest movement sets the colorful balls moving about, the toddler is excited about the actions that she causes and controls and is motivated to continue walking in a stable movement pattern.

Soft Electronic Rock 'n Bounce Pony
(Today's Kids)

Realistic galloping, trotting and snorting sounds of this bounce-along rocking horse encourage imaginative play, fantasy role-playing and active physical exercise. Combining technology with a traditional ride on-experience, the active toddler embraces the various horse sounds while training her legs, arms and torso to work in tandem to stabilize her lower body. "Riding" and then stopping this ground-level rocker further trains the toddler to use muscular control. Motivational and engaging role-play and sound effects encourages confidence and independent play. Many pretend scenarios can be formulated while bouncing on this soft pony.

Jumbo Music Block
(Neurosmith)

Children love to investigate and discover. This multi-task learning environment engages children and entertains them with music and motor activities while reinforcing shape learning and language skills. Each side of this soft, oversized block features zippers, snaps and buttons for dexterity and daily living skills. There are secret pockets to uncover, books to look at and even shiny mirrors for a quick game of peek-a-boo. Baby can lean on this block or even play in a prone position over it. The four-sided music makes the block particularly stimulating as each side transforms into a distinct play environment.

Dunk & Clunk Circus Rings
(Sassy)

The toddler is challenged when fitting pieces into this shape sorter and then proudly observing her accomplishments. Multi-textured rings slip into special slots through the lid of this see-through, plastic container. These rings provide stimulating visual and tactile experiences and, as they drop, they motivate interaction and encourage the development of hold and release behaviors. This activity fosters size discrimination and problem solving proficiency. Simple sorting tasks like these are important underpinnings of later learning and school success and also refine attention, finger dexterity, perceptual awareness, motor learning and abstract thinking skills.

Stack 'N Learn Sorter
(LEGO)

As toddlers stack and fit rounded shapes together, they explore a variety of spatial relationships, color matching and recognition and the concept of trial and error. Tasks such as stacking and balancing set the stage for problem solving and learning about color, shape and size. Items can be stacked in a tower, dropped into a shape sorter or played with separately. Through manipulation, the child discovers how to predict size and fit and, while doing so, she can experiment with how things are similar and different. Since tower building also requires the ability to perceive continuity and size, this activity center provides many challenges and learning opportunities.

Crazy Legs Bug
(VTech)

This roll-along pull-toy features a character with six shape-sorter extensions that teaches forms, letter identification and colors. In addition to promoting large and small motor skill development and independent play, the noises and music that accompany the toy's action sharpen listening and concentration skills. A variety of learning activities keep the toddler busy and fully engaged in interacting with this product. Separate actions allow each youngster to utilize this toy in her own unique way. And, since the shapes are attached to the toy in the form of legs, there are no loose pieces or missing parts to interfere with play.

Sparkling Symphony Drum-Along Bear
(Fisher-Price)

As the child refines her walking and running abilities, she receives constant feedback from the toy following close behind her. Active toddlers can develop many competencies when playing with a pull toy, including a measured running pace, directionality, balance and large motor coordination. This product includes additional reinforcement for physical effort, as sparkling lights, spinning stars and a flutter ball offer extra visual stimulation and motivation. As toddlers improve their steadiness and balance, this pull toy can lead them to new physical challenges. Practicing walking at a quick pace activates this product, but it also keeps movement controlled, focused and purposeful. And, security is built when the child knows her toy companion remains with her in new situations.

Quack Along Ducks
(Tomy)

This traditional pull toy enhances large motor skills and encourages continuous upright movement. The toddler is greeted by gentle "quacking" as she pulls along a mother duck and her little green and yellow ducklings waddling behind her. Great toys encourage and motivate children to participate in developmentally appropriate activities. Practicing walking and running engages the toddler and challenges her ability to control her movement and continuous motor development. This participation reinforces balance and coordination as she plans and organizes her movements to accommodate the "ducks" behind her.

PART 2: TOYS FOR TODDLERS

TOYS FOR THE 18-24 MONTH-OLD

TOYS FOR THE 2 -YEAR -OLD

IV

Chapter 4: Toys for 18-to 24 -Month Olds

Within a period of a few short months, the physically active baby is transformed into a highly mobile and coordinated toddler who can run, balance, push, pull and climb. Much of her time and energy is devoted to practicing and refining large-motor skills and demonstrating increasingly complex physical aptitudes.   In addition to her own constant motion, her fascination with movement is reflected in her play preferences for toys with many moving parts and small shifting objects.

This developmental period is characterized by enormous growth in cognitive and linguistics skills as well as physical abilities. During these months, short and long-term memory improves dramatically, as evidenced by the popularity of games like hide and seek. The toddler's expanded capacity to retain and recall information is demonstrated by her pleasure in asking and searching for objects that are no longer within her range of vision. Language acquisition is also rapid, as many children will try to put words together in meaningful ways to create short phrases. It is not unusual for the toddler's 10-word vocabulary to expand to 200 words by her second birthday. In addition to her use of words, her gestures and facial expressions also signal an increased understanding of the art of communication.

Even before play experiences are truly cooperative, physical proximity to other children during play can facilitate interaction. This type of "parallel play" is developmentally important, although it may seem as if the child notices nothing – and no one – but herself.

Prior to social play with peers, the toddler's actions are egocentric, and all about "me". As the child approaches her second birthday, however, she often becomes more responsive to siblings and peers during play and better able to assert her own self in a group situation. During this developmental stage, words like "mine" and "no" echo through the halls of day care centers. Beloved toys become favored possessions that cannot be shared! The act of distinguishing these favorite and special items from all others is important. It reflects the child's attempt to establish an identity that is different from that of her mother. She is now ready to begin the development of autonomy. Playthings that are appropriate for the young toddler are:

Tidoo
(Corolle)

A special doll provides an important nurturing connection and an emotional anchor for the young child. At the core of role-playing, a baby doll can help a child to express her emotions. As a caregiver for pretend "doll children", children gain self-awareness and develop empathy and compassion. This doll actually responds to tender loving care, and does so in *living color*! Red "boo-boos" and "measles" are washed away with warm water and the doll's rosy cheeks even disappear when she is inside and out of the cold. Baby Tidoo is also a reliable playmate for the bath – but, watch out … If her bathing suit turns red, it means the bath water is too hot!

 Visual

 Tactile

 Social

Sing With Me Magic Cube
(Munchkin)

Music can enrich a child's environment and stimulate her sensory awareness. The inquisitive toddler is aware of the music around her and she will enjoy listening to this musical cube while focusing her attention, memory and interest. Listening skills are reinforced as some of the best loved songs like "Old McDonald", "Itsy Bitsy Spider", "BINGO" and "Pop Goes the Weasel" are orchestrated and played. This product actually puts the child in the conductor's seat with the simple push of a button. Children can add on instruments or take them away, thereby building sound combinations and patterns and recognizing each instrument for the sound it contributes.

 Cognitive

 Auditory

 Creativity

35

Tolo Animal Water Slide
(Small World)

Suctioned to the tub, this shape sorter comes with circle, square and triangle water scoops. But, in addition to traditional bath play and puzzle activities, this toy can also help the child focus on cause and effect relationships. When the bath lever is pressed, animal rafts slide and splash into the bath water. This tub toy keeps play exciting and helps the toddler to develop her imagination and small motor coordination. As she bathes, the young child actively participates in independent play and develops self-confidence and autonomy. Interesting bath toys enhance the examination and exploration of water and facilitate discovery and learning.

Maxi Modo Blocks
(Chicco)

Building with bocks stimulates perceptual and motor skills and teaches problem solving strategies. Through trial and error with blocks, children sharpen their perceptual awareness and finger and hand dexterity. The connection between the development of perceptual abilities and cognitive skills is strong and soft blocks can introduce and reinforce this important connection. They can also provide opportunities to solve problems and see new size relationships. These large, soft blocks can be used during individual or group play ensuring that a first building experience is enjoyable, educational and successful.

Music 'N Lights Sit 'N Spin
(Playskool)

As she turns two, the young child's need for physical activity is almost constant and her supply of energy, practically endless! This product can be used individually or by two youngsters in tandem. It assists in the exploration of spinning and gives toddlers an opportunity to channel their physical energy in a focused manner. While sitting on this product, the youngster utilizes her hands and arms and upper body muscles to propel a circular disk. She is able to achieve a pleasurable spinning sensation as well as independently control the speed and intensity of the motion. Active participation, strength building and cooperative play are reinforced and flashing lights and recorded songs reward the child.

Tap 'N Turn Bench
(Fisher-Price)

Young builders pound and hammer while reinforcing their strength and eye-hand coordination. Through this "real work" task, the concepts of shape sorting, hammering, color differentiation and cause and effect relationships are introduced and an important sense of accomplishment is experienced. Pounding down colorful pegs and then flipping the bench over with ready anticipation to begin the process again is an age-old favorite play activity of toddlers. And, while the child is working to complete her efforts, the peg's colors and shapes are becoming familiar as well. This toy provides opportunities for eye-hand development and small motor coordination.

Learning Hoops
(LeapFrog)

This tot-sized basketball hoop introduces the active toddler to the world of letters, numbers and words. The realistic voice of a basketball announcer, crowd cheers and music further motivates interaction and play with this product. Multi-media enhanced play and full participation in learning create excitement for inquisitive learners. Lights on a backboard flash when baby scores, motivating her to continue the learning process. Hands-on, engaging activities supplement pre-reading and pre-math early childhood skill-building activities. Exposure to various preschool concepts during play enables the child to feel comfortable when they are presented in a more formal school setting.

Gazoobo
(Chicco)

When the curious child opens the color-coded door with the corresponding color-coded key, she will be greeted by a friendly animal and feel proud of her ability. This is a multi-level activity toy with geometric shapes to sort and animal blocks to enrich fantasy play. The introduction of keys is particularly interesting for young children and highlights their fascination with functional tools. Large keys encourage small motor coordination and there are numerous other sensory motor opportunities experienced by youngsters as they play with this product. Importantly, youngsters feel successful as they master each opening of this product independently.

38

Little Red Roadster
(Radio Flyer)

This classic foot-to-floor car has a sturdy steel body, working steering wheel and steel wheels with real rubber tires. Young drivers are able to steer within a small range and control speed and direction with their feet. Maneuvering independently in a realistic vehicle enhances a child's self esteem and feelings of competency. Controlling the speed and direction of the roadster from "the driver's seat" supports strategic motor planning, concentration and responsibility. Driving also reinforces coordination both in managing various body parts working together and in responding to visual stimuli with the correct bodily reactions.

Step Start Walk 'N Ride
(Playskool)

When children are walking and running with some steadiness, they may be ready to enjoy the freedom and control of a stable, low to the ground, easily straddled and steered ride-on toy. Propelling the vehicle by pushing with both feet simultaneously is a method for moving swiftly and independently. As the toddler maneuvers this vehicle, she gains a sense of control and accomplishment. And, as she manages turns and balancing, she also develops large motor skills and lower body strength. This toy converts from a push toy to a ride-on using a parent-activated locking mechanism.

Discovery Sounds Playstore
(Little Tikes)

"Shopping" in this vibrant interactive store inspires fantasy play and adult imitation. A stimulating environment for role-playing, this grocery market contains a number of manipulative, role-playing and socialization activities. The cash register has large buttons to push and can make silly noises. Colorful money shapes fit into a working drawer and the fruit shaped balls race down a ramp and land in a shopping basket. Pretend fruit, cheese and milk shapes drop through a countertop sorter and into a shopping basket. This process fosters fantasy and imitation and encourages goal-directed behavior.

Bath Puppets
(Baby Einstein)

Sitting still in the bath and staying focused on the task of bathing can be challenging for the young child. These puppets can be helpful as they assist in washing and managing soap while also bringing fun and purposeful activity to the bath environment. For some toddlers, puppets can be particularly useful if children are fearful of water and the bathtub. Puppets make imaginative bath toys and foster dramatic play. Both in and outside of the water, these puppets can facilitate discovery and learning. As she bathes, the young child participates in language-rich fantasy play and reinforces developing language skills through puppetry play.

40

Push-Along Block Cart
(Ryan's Room Small World)

Traditional hardwood blocks help toddlers learn to classify by size, shape and color. Block play introduces concepts such as longer, shorter, higher, behind and over or under and reinforces language learning and shape identification in the process. Relationships such as big, bigger and biggest are important pre-numerical models and are especially meaningful to children when they are discovered during play. Attention to similarities and differences and awareness of balance and small motor planning are fundamental lessons in block building. This special set of blocks forms a large three-dimensional puzzle in its own push-along cart.

Aquini Drink and Wet Bath Babies
(Gotz)

Play props are extremely helpful in developing children's social skills. For many activities of daily living, particularly in the area of personal hygiene, relevant behaviors can be introduced and illustrated using toys that transform into social learning props. This doll has a sealed vinyl body that makes it a practical bath toy and an easy-to-use toilet training aide. During bath play, potty training can be acted out using an anatomically correct doll, such as this, that actually drinks and "wets". Learning through play is both effective and fun and can be a valuable resource in gaining social competencies.

John Deere Toy Push Lawn Mower
(Ertl)

The toddler may feel discouraged over her inability to control many of the larger, adult sized activities and objects in her environment. Tot-sized replicas of familiar objects and the role-playing of everyday activities can instill feelings of competence and security. As the youngster gains a sense of control and participation in the world, she is better able to confront new situations and be comfortable with her own size and abilities. Aspiring to be "just like mom" or "just like dad" can be reinforced in appropriate fantasy play. This lawnmower push toy makes realistic lawnmower sounds and even includes pretend grass that swirls around a clear chamber while the child is pushing the mower.

Amazing Baby Touch And Play!
(Silver Dolphin Books)

This tactile reading experience combines the activity of texture play with reading readiness. Baby's first books are "hands-on" opportunities for learning as she touches shapes, textures and even discovers directional concepts! An activity play book, this tactile learning vehicle is an important component of early concept formation and introduces the young child to the reading process. As baby turns the pages of this book, she will use her fingers to explore and learn.

V

Chapter 5: Toys for Two-Year-Olds

The language development process has three distinct elements - a child's innate capacity to speak words, motivation to communicate and the ability to imitate behavior. When communication is enhanced by a highly verbal environment language acquisition is rapidly established. This process is easily observed in the social interactions of the 2-year-old. During this spurt in talking and language development, opportunities for conversation and verbal play are extremely important.

In addition to strides made in the area of language, improved mental and physical ability reveal a readiness for advanced toys that challenge dexterity and eye-hand coordination. Observation and inspection of objects and an analysis of how things work is particularly keen for this group. Play pieces that can be easily fitted together and taken apart will reinforce the toddler's fine motor skills and ability to focus attention. She is likely to become frustrated by objects that require extensive manipulation or that are too complicated or too large to control. Toys, sporting equipment and play props should be scaled to the child's size as well as her current interests and abilities.

The 2-year-old demonstrates surprising strength, agility and physical coordination. She can now adjust her running speed, jump with both feet, walk backwards and tiptoe. She is able to push and pull wheeled objects and steer ride-on toys. Playthings that encourage rigorous activity will assist in the development of general coordination and large motor proficiency.

As the child approaches 3, she engages in continuous interaction with the world as she investigates, discovers, predicts and invents through the vehicle of play. Trying new things – both physical and cognitive – will enable the child to learn experientially - by "doing." During this time, the foundation for group experiences, socialization activities and learning strategies necessary for success in a nursery or pre-school environment are established.

Experiences during which the toddler can fantasize, lead, participate, cooperate and succeed are effective preparation for a school setting and a powerful foundation for later learning. The following toys are recommended for 2-year olds and were selected to reflect the natural curiosity and increasing self-awareness of these youngsters:

Familiar Things
(Lauri)

Between the ages of two and three, children enjoy doing simple inset puzzles. Increasing proficiency with "fitting" pieces into puzzles is a result of improved visual and perceptual skills, memory and small motor coordination. With each solution, the young child refines early trial and error strategies and gains perceptual awareness and confidence. This classic double - thick puzzle set is easy for young children to manipulate, and the colorful, recognizable shapes help beginners develop matching skills and small-motor abilities. This product is made from a soft material that allows youngsters to actually squeeze puzzle pieces into place.

Little People Home Sweet Home
(Fisher-Price)

Miniature environments help children arrange and direct a world of fantasy. Perhaps the most recognizable and comfortable environment for acting out familiar roles is the setting of a home. This house and family are stimulating props that facilitate important pretend play. The house is detailed with features that even include a 21st century nursery monitor that plays baby sounds and lullabies, a refrigerator door that opens and a toilet seat that lifts. The "Little People" and their furniture are sized appropriately for the young child's developing grasp and coordination.

Made For Me! Talking Cell Phone
(Hasbro)

Toy telephones are among children's most favored props for imaginative play. In addition to the telephone's role playing value, language and listening skills are practiced with a familiar and fun tool. And, since toddlers love to mimic grown-up conversations, fantasy play with the latest cell phone expands social abilities and awareness. This phone has a ring back feature along with nine recorded messages. The child can talk on her phone while imitating parents as they talk on their phones. While pressing buttons, there is continuous feedback and ringing and dialing. Pretend phone calls challenge perceptual and small motor coordination as well.

Complete Cook Set
(Alex)

When two-year-olds engage in the important activity of fantasy role-play, the most stimulating props are likely to be those that are child-sized and realistic. Children love to mimic adult behavior and copy things that grown-ups "do". Playtime includes imitating the physical actions of adults and copying grown-ups' use of familiar household objects. Pretend cooking with detailed and functional kitchen replicas encourages cooperative interaction, creative thinking, language and small motor skill development. This play cookware set contains pots and pans, measuring spoons and potholders for the pretend chef.

Fun Tunes Tractor
(Playskool)

This tractor sorter helps children explore classification strategies and shape and song discrimination. Child-friendly songs greet the child when the animals are placed, correctly, in the tractor. This moveable, musical puzzle entertains children and reinforces sorting and spatial relationships. A friendly farm song signals that the animals have been appropriately placed in the tractor. A pull along feature guides the active toddler as she plays.

Cozy Coupe Car
(Little Tikes)

This sturdy plastic car gives toddlers and young preschoolers the experience of driving and controlling a foot-powered car. Children sit on a bench-style driver's seat while they develop coordinated movement and large motor skills. Guiding a vehicle, especially one that looks like a real car, provides hours of fun and exercise. As the toddler begins to move her legs, the car begins to scoot forward. Stroller-like wheels make this coupe particularly responsive to the steering wheel. The front dash features a pretend key and horn that encourages fantasy play as well as coordinated motor planning opportunities, increased attention and concentration.

Tonka Trucks
(Playskool)

These durable and realistic trucks provide opportunities for sharing and group play and are associated with real work. The detail and precision of these products adds to dramatic role-playing, physical planning and building. Appropriate for indoor and outdoor activities, these classic trucks have articulated parts with motion, function and numerous real working features. Their authenticity and heavy-duty steel construction motivates rugged young construction workers and excites them with fantasy play opportunities. These trucks facilitate play with materials such as sand and dirt, enhancing their potential creativity and over all "play value."

Maggie Raggie Boo Boo Buddies
(Zapf)

Accident-prone toddlers will enjoy playing with these soft-bodied girl and boy dolls, designed with unique therapeutic functions. Each multi-ethnic "buddy" boasts a shoulder bag that doubles as a reusable cold pack for icing and numbing the pain of minor bruises, scrapes and "boo boos". The use of cold compresses or ice cubes for the reduction of an injury's swelling or to lower a toddler's fever can be an unpleasant experience for a young child. The colorful cold pack with the comfort of a friendly doll, however, is a child-friendly, and even welcomed healing alternative.

Pretend & Learn Shopping Cart
(LeapFrog)

This interactive shopping cart combines the elements of a push toy with an electronic pre-school teaching product. Through imitation of familiar scenes and grocery shopping behaviors, children rehearse the roles of parents and shoppers while improving their cognitive, social and motor skills. This innovative, educational and socialization prop encourages imaginative play. It includes high-tech devices that maximize the developmental learning experience. A realistic electronic scanner recognizes each food item as children are introduced to age-appropriate concepts such as more than/less than, food groups and shopping for healthy vegetables.

Medical Kit
(Fisher-Price)

Playing doctor remains a popular and important role in the fantasy play of children. Preschoolers often have concerns about their bodies, potential injuries and health and about visiting the doctor. Role-playing these concerns provides the comfort of knowing just what to expect and this doctor's kit will help young patients better understand what going to the doctor entails. Acting out a visit to the doctor develops a child's imagination and helps her gain new insight, confidence and an enhanced sense of control. Importantly, this fantasy play allows her to rehearse a potentially stressful activity in a safe and familiar environment.

49

First Shape Fitter
(BRIO)

This 3-dimensional puzzle helps the young learner participate in concrete, "hands-on" experiences with pre-school concepts and stretch their concentration and attention abilities. By matching assorted shapes with the same shape's receptacle on boxes, children are exposed to the various similarities and differences of objects. As children fit objects into the correct spaces provided, they are increasingly motivated to continue the successful completion of this fit and drop task. This shape sorter provides opportunities to develop eye-hand coordination, compare the look and feel of various forms, their relative sizes and relationships and provides an introduction to basic geometric shapes.

Toss n' Play Activity Set
(Learning Resources)

A beanbag toss and a hop around a large floor mat makes learning numbers, shapes and colors fun. Big movements help to develop coordination, balance and large motor skills. Various games can be played whereby players are sent out to land on a particular color or number on the mat. Jumping into a particular box or even staying off the lines can sharpen a young child's perceptual and motor abilities as well as her ability to listen and follow directions. And the competitive use of a play mat makes exercise and movement fun as well as challenging.

Zoo Knuckleheads
(Mary Meyer)

These 4-inch finger puppets are designed for little fingers to move with dramatic expression. Communication and story telling is enriched through puppet play and imaginative thinking is reinforced. Finger puppets can aid in socialization and promote interaction between children at play. Solitary play can also be enhanced by puppetry and drama, particularly when the fantasy element of role-playing and puppets are combined. Play with finger puppets can increase finger and hand dexterity and sharpen eye-hand coordination. The development of small motor skills and dramatic performance are ongoing and encouraged by finger and hand activity.

Buggsy
(Aurora)

A colorful caterpillar with six legs and six interactive features educates and entertains. While sharpening important small motor skills, finger dexterity and general coordination are reinforced. Each leg of this stuffed animal features a rattle, snap or Velcro strap, so the toddler is continuously challenged and amused. Small motor abilities are precursors to numerous daily living skills, and dolls that double as small-motor skill builders can provide additional exposure and small motor practice. Children who will need additional time to master self-help and dressing activities may gain valuable extra practice with toys such as this.

51

PART 3: TOYS FOR PRESCHOOLERS

TOYS FOR THE 3-YEAR-OLD

TOYS FOR THE 4-YEAR -OLD

VI

Chapter 6: Toys for Three-Year-Olds

The core characteristic of the active toddler's social learning and expression is imitation. It is no surprise, therefore, that many of the future roles of adulthood are naturally rehearsed and acted out during symbolic or "pretend" play. Between the ages of 3 and 4, shared fantasy becomes a major part of role-playing behavior and group socialization. This creative interaction further enriches the language component of play and the early childhood experience.

During preschool years, the role of dolls, toy cars, blocks, and work-oriented props becomes increasingly important in setting the stage for future development and learning. These toys allow children to safely and comfortably try out new roles and behaviors, solve fundamental problems and experiment with taking responsibility. These items can also facilitate expressions of affection, joy and anger and stimulate verbal communication.

Appropriate play experiences during this developmental period include activities that refine a variety of cognitive and motor skills and prepare youngsters for more complex learning. These "readiness' activities are not designed to push academics or squeeze the fun out of playtime - they simply introduce concepts like letters, words, stories and numbers in an atmosphere filled with success, security and fun. The challenge at this time is not to actually *teach* reading and math, but rather to reinforce important requisite skills and instill favorable attitudes and enthusiasm toward learning.

Play offers 3-year olds experience with abstractions, anticipating consequences and planning and executing tasks. Among those toys especially recommend for this age group are:

Kiddie Kick Scooter
(Razor)

This "tot-sized" scooter allows the pre-school rider to develop her small and large muscle groups while moving quickly and having fun. As she directs her physical actions, she is building muscular strength and agility and increasing her endurance. Used for building leg muscles, endurance and speed, this scooter was designed for the smallest and youngest users with a balanced base and additional training wheels for stability and safety. As the child pushes and glides, the lightweight construction and three-wheel design assist her in balancing, controlling and steering. Foam handgrips additionally provide security and control and help the child feel successful and confident while riding.

Tikes Patrol Police Car
(Little Tikes)

Practice driving and steering reinforces perceptual and motor coordination. Guiding a vehicle -- especially one that has realistic car features-- provides hours of physical activity, perceptual training and fun. This blue squad car has an electronic microphone with seven different emergency siren sounds and runs on foot power. When fantasy role-playing is combined with focused physical activities, youngsters become fully engaged in the play process. As preschoolers learn to moderate and control their actions they develop important play skills and socialization strategies.

Little People Discovery Airport
(Fisher-Price)

Early role-playing experiences are important and using the tools of a pretend world to practice the roles of adulthood can enhance and enrich development. Children are fascinated by transportation and the excitement of airplanes and airports. This play environment, complete with figures and vehicles, helps the child create a fantasy environment in which she can make decisions and play many roles. While interacting with others and playing with the airport, preschoolers develop predictable outcomes and a sense of security and self-confidence. While imitating real-world experiences in fantasy play, children are able to act out their fears and anxieties within a safe and protected environment.

Kid K'NEX
(K'NEX)

These pre-school building sets were especially designed to meet the needs of the three-year-old builder and to limit any unnecessary frustration that might be encountered because of small fingers or limited dexterity. These free-form sets make use of a simple connection mechanism that enables young builders to complete constructions independently. The system utilizes brightly colored plastic that easily and securely combine with one another. As the child designs, builds and plays with her constructions, she increases her visual and spatial awareness and refines her manual dexterity. The completed product is a comic character that can double as a "toy pal", providing a sense of accomplishment and self-worth.

Squeak E. Mouse Gets Dressed
(International Playthings)

At this developmental stage, children are motivated to learn the skills necessary for independent dressing. Although children's ability to perform small motor tasks – and their eye-hand coordination, finger dexterity and ability to tie and button – will vary greatly, attempts to practice self-help tasks and skills of every day living should be encouraged. This dressing mouse is a fun way to introduce dressing skills while providing practice for the fine motor challenges of buttoning, zippering, buckling, tying and snapping. When the preschooler is motivated and capable, she will appreciate opportunities to perform and rehearse these activities of daily living on her own.

Classic Tricycle
(Radio Flyer)

Between a child's third and fourth birthdays, her increased strength, flexibility and agility enable her to graduate from a push to a pedal vehicle. This classic three-wheeled tricycle has a sturdy steel construction and a double-deck rear step. A 12" front wheel contributes to a balanced and stable ride for the new driver. Other important features of this bike include steel spoked wheels with rubber tires, streamers, and a ringing bell. In addition to fun and exercise, numerous perceptual and motor skills are reinforced as the preschooler learns to ride and control an age-appropriate bike.

My Dollhouse Completely Furnished
(Alex)

Miniature environments enable the child to arrange and direct a world of fantasy. This three-story house has one large room on each floor and one side completely open for play. Everything is included right down to the baby and the baby carriage. Many pieces of furniture have working drawers or doors and there are even lamps and computers. With these props, storylines can be developed, family roles can be explored and dramatic conflicts resolved. Pretend play expands the preschooler's imagination and creativity while social, emotional and language skills are nurtured.

Musini
(Neurosmith)

The experience of controlling music, tempo and rhythm empowers children to affect the world around them. This innovative system converts the vibrations made by clapping hands, tapping feet and other movement into musical compositions for dancing and creative movement. This auditory control stimulates physical expression and encourages coordination and creativity. Children's listening and concentration abilities are enhanced through this musical expression and feedback. In addition to reinforcing feelings of control over the volume and rhythm of the music, children enjoy the physical exercise and free-form movement that this musical toy inspires.

My Fist RC Dump Truck
(Kid Galaxy)

Controlling the function, speed and direction of a radio-controlled vehicle challenges a child's visual and motor coordination while building feelings of self-esteem and competency. By pressing the simple drive button, the child operates a moving force with the touch of a finger. This set also comes with boulders and barricades so traffic will not interfere with the work of the dump truck or the child's development of perceptual and behavior-modeling skills. While playing with the truck and other construction characters, the child can change directionality and send the truck off for another pick-up. And, simple navigation with remote control supports strategic motor planning, concentration and responsibility.

Right Height Tee Ball
(Today's Kids)

Batting practice can assist the child in achieving balance and integration on both sides of her body. Numerous perceptual and motor skills are sharpened while holding and swinging a bat. With a minimal amount of frustration, this item can introduce the skills and behaviors necessary for children to compete and succeed in sports. Important socialization and cooperation activities can also be highlighted in a tee-ball practice setting. This tee is flexible, and snaps back into position every time it is hit. Adjustable to 9 different heights, girls and boys can build confidence and skill during play.

Explore Blocks
(LEGO)

Children experience success with limited frustration while building with this creative plastic model system. Designed for pre-school builders, large pieces link together firmly, facilitating interlocking and construction. In addition to open-ended building opportunities, children explore balance, math concepts, color recognition, physical coordination, cooperation and even story telling. As children connect, pretend and design, they broaden their creative abilities and flexibility. These creative thinking skills are necessary for problem solving. Pieces can be combined in an infinite number of ways making each building experience a new adventure.

Cookin' Sounds Gourmet Kitchen
(Little Tikes)

Socialization and cooking skills are enhanced as young chefs prepare gourmet dinners in this child-sized, state of the art kitchen. Filled with realistic food-preparation features and sounds, children enjoy pretending and playing with props. A stovetop grill makes cooking noises and has light-up "flames", and as dishes are "washed," the sound of water running and dishes rattling can be heard. These functional replicas of familiar household objects and actions help children to feel comfortable in a play setting and provide them with a context for meaningful and creative fantasy play.

John Deere Tractor With Trailer
(Peg-Perego)

Between the ages of three and four, improved perceptual and motor coordination and increased lower body strength make this an appropriate time to combine peddle biking with the fantasy play elements of a "working" vehicle. This dirt hauling tractor and trailer has authentic looking parts for role-playing behavior associated with real work. Steering and riding this traditional farm vehicle inspires purposeful outdoor play and focused physical activity. Large tractor wheels help young riders safely navigate any terrain and an adjustable seat allows children of various heights to pedal with optimal footing and traction.

Goodnight Moon Game
(Briarpatch)

This early learning game assists children in visual memory, matching and manual dexterity. Based on the beloved children's book, "Goodnight Moon," between one and four players act to match familiar items from the Goodnight Moon room with individual item picture cards. Even young, pre-reading children can enjoy playing the game, taking turns and engaging in a real game strategy. These matching activities also develop and promote visual awareness and increase attention and concentration skills. In addition, these reading readiness games serve as a foundation for later letter and word recognition skills and language learning.

The Nick Jr. Sing-Along
(Singing Machine Co.)

A sing-along cassette player and a personal microphone make this "first" karaoke machine a confidence builder and socialization booster. In addition to the familiar characters and music, this product uses popular songs from the child's most beloved television programs to support singing that is sure to raise some real crowd appreciation. The special appeal of the characters and songs will motivate the 3-year-old to fully participate in the musical activity and "sing along". Since she has trust in these characters, coping with shyness and/or performance issues will most likely not stand in her way of the fun!

Auditory

Social

Cognitive

VII

Chapter 7: Toys for Four-Year-Olds

The intensity that active and curious 4-year-olds demonstrate in their play is reflected in their interest in the world around them. Exploring different aspects of their environment provides numerous opportunities for collecting items that represent the fascinating things they have done and places they have been. Toys are "collected" in a similar way and serve as important attachments and special possessions. Since favored playthings are still viewed by young children as extensions of themselves, traveling with a special toy can ease the transition between home and school or mother and caregiver. A sentimental doll or play set can communicate feelings of safety and familiarity in an unknown setting.

Improved eye-hand coordination enables the preschooler to participate in more sophisticated puzzle, construction and sports activities. She can put this enhanced dexterity to good use when building bridges or categorizing small pieces. And, she can also reinforce practical self-help and dressing skills while fostering independence.

Activities that promote creativity and integrate perceptual, motor and cognitive skills help the 4-year old who can now handle drawing and writing tools and other pre-school materials. During this year, many youngsters sharpen their non-verbal communication proficiency and communicate with letters, numbers, words, phrases and detailed pictures.

Drawing and writing are fun activities that reinforce readiness skills needed for classroom participation very shortly.

As youngsters create their unique and independent view of the world and begin to distinguish between fantasy and reality, pretend play becomes more varied, imaginative and complex. Children between 4 and 5 have already had many experiences that they can bring to role-playing exercises and an astounding large vocabulary of between 1,500 and 2,000 words to expand the possibilities for interactive play. Through participation in "make believe," empathy and self-confidence are developed and a channel for sharing feelings and solving problems is achieved.

Among the greatest strides made by 4-year-olds is that of socialization in a preschool environment, be it a nursery, day care center or playgroup. Preschool provides opportunities for peer interaction that may not be available in a child's individual home. The first school experience should be a secure transitional point between the comfort and familiarity of home and the large, new school environment. By gently exposing children to new adults, cooperative play situations and challenging readiness activities, children will be better able to handle the later demands of a classroom setting and membership and leadership within a group. Playthings recommended for children between 4 and 5 years of age are:

LeapPad
(LeapFrog)

This interactive learning center enables children to learn to read at their own pace. A system of real paper books and extensions introduce letter sounds, words and stories as they instill reading aspirations and positive attitudes toward learning. Children follow along as each word in the book is electronically read to them. Since this innovative technology includes an interactive "magic pen" that works like a hand-held computerized pointer, the child can point to any word on the page and actually hear it pronounced. The pre-reader can also touch a picture and hear its special sound as well as receive related information and activities over the Internet on her home computer.

Police Outfit and Equipment Bag "Dress-Up"
(Lillian Vernon/Lilly's Kids)

Dress up is more than fun - it is experimentation with the roles and rules of adulthood. Acting out parts and providing a safe opportunity to try out some familiar grown-up behavior is an important socialization activity for preschoolers. Through "make believe", the youngster learns how to engage in cooperative play and gains important experience in dealing with others. Fantasy play fosters creativity and imagination, but it also stimulates the investigation of specific roles and jobs. Dress up allows the youngster to feel just like the character she is pretending to be, and realistic costumes - such as this policeperson and community helper - facilitate that behavior. This outfit includes a child-sized vinyl vest, badge, hat and even sunglasses!

Happy Family
(Mattel)

This doll set features a mother, father, toddler son, baby daughter and even a baby doctor. It includes all of the realistic props necessary for fantasy play revolving around the dynamics of a young family's life. Children can pretend to take on nurturing roles and parenting responsibilities and help to introduce and integrate the brand new baby into the family. Children will benefit from dealing with the sibling rivalry issues that a new baby coming into a family presents, and do so in a safe and controlled play setting. Articulated play props including car seats and bottle warmers add rich detail to the fantasy environment.

Teaching Cash Register
(Learning Resources)

This interactive cash register makes the fun of shopping educational! A real working calculator that communicates through a large LCD display also enhances pretend play. Combined with this high-tech cash register, talking scanner and pretend credit card, appropriate in-store behaviors and arithmetic and money skills are taught and reinforced. In addition to enhancing fantasy role-play, children learn the recognition and usage of realistic coins, making change and other simple calculations. Play helps the child understand the cost of a purchase and the true value of money.

Classic Railway
(BRIO)

Classic small wooden trains operate on child power and are one of the most favored playthings of preschoolers. This durable set facilitates group interaction as well as independent play. Children enjoy creating train stories and characters while engaging in track building, problem solving and pretend play. As children maneuver the train around the track, they learn about magnets, reinforce eye-hand coordination and enrich language and socialization skills. A flexible play experience that can adjust to the needs and abilities of the individual youngster, a simple activity like this can be a springboard for elaborate fantasy scenarios.

Jr. Shave And Play Kit
(Small World Toys)

In the safe environment of fantasy and the security of home, children experiment with pretend roles and imitate their parents' behaviors. Modeling the actions of adults help youngsters to imprint activities that adults "do" and visualize what they aspire to become. Through observation, the child learns to perform certain activities and this learning is reinforced through practice and play. Other language and social interaction skills improve during the process. This simple "pretend" shaving kit was made especially for young children who need support in areas of confidence and self-esteem.

Playmobil Airport
(Playmobil)

The miniature world of a themed play set offers numerous opportunities for social learning and symbolic play. As the child interacts with this realistic airport scene, her imagination and creativity intensifies. These tiny, recognizable objects enhance fantasy role-playing by providing detailed figures and props that are perfectly designed for a four-year-old's interests, physical maturity and manipulative skills. These durable and articulated play sets are a stimulating means of encouraging group socialization or independent play. Children will enjoy building a "make believe" world around this airport tower, which includes everything from a check-in counter with an attendant, to a baggage carousel complete with luggage.

Tinkertoy Classic Construction Set
(Playskool)

This simple wooden building system can provide hours of open-ended, creative and unstructured play. Children love to take things apart and put them back together in new creative ways. As she constructs and designs, the young builder can experiment with joining together and taking apart elements such as spools, rods, flags and string. An endless series of combinations allows examination of balance, weight and structure. Building opportunities present numerous problem solving and perceptual tasks. Open-ended projects can support creative expression and encourage independent and focused play.

Make Silly Hats
(Creativity For Kids)

This arts activity set includes all the materials necessary for creating unique and outrageous hats inspired by Dr. Seuss's "Cat in the Hat". Linking a favorite book character to imaginative, "open-ended" play can be both instructional and fun for the developing preschooler. While youngsters challenge their ingenuity and role-play imaginary and comical situations, they improve their confidence as well as language and social skills. And, while experimenting with a range of manipulative materials - from pipe-cleaners to a pinwheel - children set the stage for rich fantasy and important pretend play. Youngsters enjoy silly themes and are proud to use props that they themselves have created.

Grow To Pro Learn To Hit Baseball
(Fisher-Price)

Learning to play baseball involves coordination and cooperation. Four–year-olds may be motivated to play, but may still be developing the skills necessary to use a bat and ball with competency and success. A secure foundation of perceptual motor ability and eye-hand coordination can be developed over time with a parent's involvement and commitment to practice. A baseball training device can be a helpful tool in promoting technique and ability. This product includes a spike with a tethered ball attached. When the child hits the ball, the parent can easily catch it with a Velcro glove. This item is particularly effective at minimizing a child's frustration while learning to play a sport.

Cranium Cadoo
(Cranium)

In this game of matching, connections reinforce short-term memory, visual discrimination and concentration. During play, preschool fundamentals -- including alphabet and number recognition and shape and color differentiation -- are presented in a challenging way and then taught and reinforced. In addition to problem solving behaviors, children learn to cooperate, focus their attention and patiently wait their turn. Best played with two to four children, this game is geared to the attention span of a four-year-old and incorporates many of the elements that young players enjoy, such as secret doors and hidden treasures.

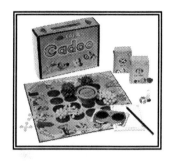

 Cognitive Visual Pre - K

Construction Jack
(Link Innovations)

Wearing hard hats, tool belts, safety glasses and overalls, these 12" dolls provide a positive and non-violent alternative to traditional action figures. In the character of hard working, "blue collar" workers, these figures familiarize youngsters with the work of people in the trades and celebrate their contribution to society. While boys and girls play with these detailed and amply costumed representatives of the painting, plumbing, carpentry and electrical trades, they learn about the actual work, responsibilities and equipment of trades people and gain an understanding and respect of their efforts. Through this active doll play, children also refine their own language, communication and role-playing skills.

 Creativity Social Cognitive

Lincoln Logs
(K'NEX)

These traditional wooden building components stack easily and rest securely, making them particularly appropriate for 4-year-old builders. Inserts in each log facilitate assembly and, when fitted together, log cabins, forts and other interesting structures can be created. Unlike completely "open ended" construction toys, children can create familiar environments that foster adaptation and socialization. While following simple assembly directions, the child gains experience in sequencing, following directions and map and chart reading. Creating a recognizable structure helps a child gain self-confidence and a sense of accomplishment and self worth.

KidStarts Treadmill
(Sport Fun)

Developing the foundation for a healthy and active lifestyle begins early in life. Youngsters should be encouraged to be physically active and engage in regular daily exercise. Specially designed "child-scaled" exercise equipment enable the pre-schooler to develop a workout routine right alongside her parents. This children's fitness system, including a treadmill for jogging and walking, stair stepper, rowing machine and weight-lifting bench, promotes health and motion, as well as having fun. As the child directs her physical activities and schedule, she is building muscular strength, endurance and balance. And, this miniature gym equipment includes special safety adaptations for young children including weight and speed controls.

Lite Brite Cube
(Playskool)

Creating designs with light has a magical quality that stimulates a child's sensory awareness and inspires learning. This 4-panel light box encourages perceptual motor development and assists youngsters in their organization and use of space. Children can work independently or in groups to complete open-ended designs. Over 500 colorful pegs illuminate original works of art to provide a new dimension to creative play. This multi-dimensional design sculpture can be changed and rearranged or left as display. In addition to strengthening eye-hand coordination, "writing readiness" is enhanced by this product's help in developing finger- dexterity and pincer grasp.

Scream Machine Jr.
(Razor)

This lightweight, low-riding three-wheel dragster provides a stable bike ride for youngsters. The all-steel frame makes this bike extremely maneuverable and popular. The introduction of age and size-appropriate hand brakes permits the child to gain independence and enhanced stopping control. Children are thrilled to pedal with this freewheel system and challenge their muscles and motivation to bring them speed. Although the bike's construction and breaks are extremely responsive, wearing a well-fitted helmet, elbow and kneepads are always recommended.

PART 4: TOYS FOR SCHOOL-AGED CHILDREN

TOYS FOR:

CHILDREN WHO EXPERIMENT

CHILDREN WHO CREATE

CHILDREN WHO BUILD

CHILDREN WHO TRAVEL

CHILDREN WITH SPECIAL NEEDS

VIII

Chapter 8: For Children Who Experiment: Science Activity Toys

Skeptics may believe that toys considered the most "educational" are usually not the most "fun." Science toys, however, will prove these doubters wrong!

While providing amusement and enjoyment, science activity toys lead to exciting, independent discovery. Throughout this play process, children develop an understanding of scientific principles, research methods and evaluation techniques. While playing with science toys, youngsters also gain experience following directions, sequencing and building confidence.

In addition to reinforcing academic concepts, science activity toys are a valuable adjunct to other educational programs. Challenging experiments that really work fuel a child's enthusiasm for discovery and learning. This learning enriches the science curriculum and encourages further investigation. It also reveals the challenge and fun of school subjects that can be introduced and reinforced at home.

Large and varied ranges of science toys are available to help parents match specific projects and kits to the interests and abilities of their children. Exposure to these experiments in a relaxed, play atmosphere bolsters children's interest in science. Learning can take place during the most joyful and challenging play experiences.

From the Invisible Man to chemistry sets, the inspiration of science toys still burns brightly in the minds of many adult scientists and researchers. But even if play with these fascinating toys does not result in a budding scientist, the experience will encourage continued investigation and experimentation. Some of the most interesting science activity toys include the following:

StarBlast
(Orion)

Science activity toys can inspire a child's fascination with science and motivate her natural inclination to discover new things. Astronomy and space exploration, in particular, have captivated the imaginations of today's children and deepened their interests in the sciences. This child-sized, reflecting, point-and-view telescope swivels on a low-profile base and engages the young child in observing the worlds beyond. While looking through a finder scope, a 13mm (4.5") parabolic mirror allows children to clearly see the Moon's craters, planets and star clusters. Images, both beautiful and educational, will surely keep children – and their parents – enthralled.

GeoSafari Sea Search
(Educational Insights)

This challenging and advanced interactive topographical map enables the young scientist to explore oceans, discover the secret lives of sharks, whales, and giant squid and even join famous explorers, past and present, as they sail around the world. Opportunities for scientific observation and participation are provided, making this learning experience a stimulating and enriching one. There are seven game modes that highlight ocean exploration and feature MP3 speech, electronic pen point-and-touch technology and hundreds of sound effects. Diverse, intense and self-directed interests can be fostered through this exciting, interactive product.

Explore and Draw Deluxe Microscope
(Funrise Toys)

This "first" microscope will challenge the curiosity of the youngest scientist and allow her to see small worlds that previously, she could have only imagined. Simple to use multiple lenses enhance viewing and a sample disk allows close-up inspection of minuscule plant and animal life. A built-in light further illuminates the objects under investigation. This microscope is versatile and sturdy enough to be used for most beginning educational investigations and explorations. Children's curiosity about the miniature world and all that "can not be seen with the naked eye" will motivate the investigation of many household objects under the magnification of this amazing lens.

Giant Ant Farm
(Uncle Milton)

This classic "observational toy" provides an excellent introduction to insect behavior and a fascinating window into the activities of community-minded ants. As these tiny creatures are observed building roads, digging tunnels and interacting with one another, the young ant-watcher maintains interest and amusement. The study of an insect community leads to a greater understanding of the organization of other animal environments and the motivation for continued exploration of behavior and the sciences. In addition, feeding and caring for insects, animals and other living things helps young scientists develop an interest in life cycles and a sense of responsibility.

Discovery Channel View-Master Projector and Telescope
(Fisher-Price)

Children are excited to explore their world and worlds beyond from a never-before-seen and close-up perspective. This telescope expands what the eye can see and enables even preschoolers to take a closer look at the stars. Bringing distant objects into close range provides youngsters with an opportunity to examine every day items in new ways and to closely investigate the world beyond their doorstep. Exploration with a telescope conveys a wide field of view and facilitates children's interests in nature and astronomy. This product also doubles as a projector, and can transmit clear images from photo reels onto screens, walls or ceilings.

Dig It Up!-NY
(Spring International)

For the child interested in becoming a paleontologist – or just plain interested in science - this excavation kit can be engaging and educational. Realistic dinosaur fossils are embedded in a plaster block for the child to excavate and reconstruct. Eye-hand coordination, problem solving and sequencing behaviors are all reinforced as the child chips away at a plaster block with special excavation tools including a hammer and chisel. As the outline of the fossil begins to emerge, the child brushes away the loosened plaster. Once a kit is completely excavated, lacquer can be applied to the fossil so it can be displayed as a collectible.

81

Butterfly Garden
(Insect Lore)

Despite their small size, butterflies are among the world's most amazing creatures and their transformation from the life of a caterpillar to a beautiful butterfly is nothing short of miraculous. Children have a chance to see this "metamorphosis" close-up, as they view the various life stages of this interesting insect through a specially designed setting. The butterfly garden makes it possible to observe the caterpillar's transition as it matures, changes into a chrysalis and finally emerges as a butterfly. A colorful butterfly house, feeding kit, and other information on the growth and development of butterflies are also included.

Star Theater 2
(Uncle Milton)

A CD guided tour entertains and informs young scientists as they set the night sky by season, day and time. This innovative "home planetarium" visually projects thousands of stars, planets and constellations onto the walls and ceiling of a child's own room. A glow-in-the-dark sphere, illuminated by a bright halogen light, displays stars, their locations, configurations and names. Scientific information, combined with a stunning visual exhibit, makes this an excellent teaching tool. And, a hand-held "meteor marker" encourages budding astronomers to interact with the projected lights and create streaming meteors and other interstellar objects to track and follow.

Mining Kit- Gems
(Uncle JimStones)

This science activity toy combines children's curiosity about finding things in the earth with their delight in role-playing activities and personalities. By incorporating the actions of a miner – sifting through dirt with a sieve in order to find real gemstones and then collecting and categorizing the shiny stones – youngsters participate in a scientific discovery adventure. Experiencing success while engaged in activities that enable the child to participate in discovery is important. While "learning by doing", learning becomes an enjoyable process and competency and independence are reinforced.

Undersea Encounter
(Uncle Milton)

This interactive aquarium allows the young scientist to actually swim with the fish and be face-to-face with the action! An innovative viewing scope with a powerful underwater lens allows magnification of the central area of aquarium activity. In addition, a special feeding pod illuminated by the lens enables the child to closely observe and monitor the feeding and swimming patterns of goldfish, guppies and other small fish. Observing underwater adventures fosters inquisitiveness and discovery. Children obtain numerous facts and collect a wide range of information about underwater life as they observe fish in this interesting environment.

Robot Rover
(Silver Dolphin Books)

This inventor's handbook and building kit introduces the young scientist to the futuristic world of robotics and provides them with an opportunity to build their own fully functional robot. Illustrated charts, diagrams and easy-to-follow instructions accompany the basic components that include wires, an electric motor, rubber wheels, nuts and bolts and a sensor. Specialized templates familiarize children with the basics of robotics and teach them about the numerous uses that robots have in the home, business as well as in scientific investigation and in space.

IX

Chapter 9: Toys For Children Who Create: Art Activity Toys

Every youngster can benefit from involvement in the arts and enjoy experiences that foster creativity. Regardless of special ability or talent, each child has the potential to produce beautiful works of art and feel proud of them. Through participation in a creative arts activity, a child can find a meaningful vehicle for self-expression and communication.

Appropriate art activities motivate and enhance learning and promote feelings of confidence and self-esteem. For some children, particularly those youngsters whose verbal skills are not yet developed for full spoken expression or discussion, the arts can be a vehicle for communication and interaction. Arts and crafts provide every youngster with a potential area of success that can be reinforced and celebrated. Experimentation with a wide range of media and materials presents opportunities for creative and emotional development, as well as for practicing visual skills and manual dexterity. As aesthetic experiences are woven into a child's life, her learning years are continuously enriched.

Art projects should be selected to reflect the interests and maturity of the child for whom they are intended. Projects should also be introduced and adjusted for each child's unique abilities and level of dexterity. Activities should not frustrate or inhibit a youngster's creative energies and should always expand upon her own life experiences.

The way in which children approach art is as individual as the creative process itself. Often, extensive supervision and assistance is necessary, and at other times, children are self-motivated and prefer to work independently. Sometimes only constant approval, encouragement and praise will keep a child creatively on task.

Opportunities for unstructured exploration of art materials such as paint and clay should be made available along with the more structured devises and craft projects mentioned in this chapter. Appropriate art materials should support a mixture of open-ended and directed projects, enabling youngsters to develop self-confidence and experience constructive criticism. Most importantly, art experiences should be vehicles for exploration, imagination, creativity and fun. Recommended visual activity toys include:

Spirograph
(Hasbro)

Children can trace exciting patterns with this gear-driven drawing machine. Using a progression of geometric disks attached to a tracing pen, budding artists and designers can produce colorful works of art. Children are introduced to geometric relationships, color-mixing strategies and spiral configurations and can place one design upon another to create innovative works of art. Practice with this compass-like instrument improves the young artist's finger dexterity and her perceptual awareness. With many potential combinations of color and pattern, each picture is unique and distinct, supporting the child's self-confidence and creative potential.

Pottery Wheel
(Curiosity Kits)

There are few art activities as creative or challenging as molding clay into a rounded form on a pottery wheel. This powerful tool enables young sculptors to create a limitless number of clay projects, refining their small motor abilities and eye-hand coordination in the process. Clay, sponges, paint and brushes are included with this tabletop electric wheel. A foot pedal is provided to power the wheel, so both hands can be used to mold and shape and smooth the clay. In addition to the process being a satisfying one, it also challenges a child's spatial awareness and sharpens her problem-solving skills.

Artist Easel With Tray Supplies
(Alex)

Children benefit from tools and materials that make painting the imaginative and creative form of self-expression that it can be. When equipment is accessible, frustration-free and age- and size-appropriate, the creative process can be a more meaningful experience. And it is the process, rather than the product that underscores the benefits of all art activities for youngsters. This well-designed, double-sided easel helps children enjoy the advantages of creative expression on an upright surface. Other practical and child-friendly design features include a built-in paper towel holder and chalkboard. Utilizing this product, children can learn to experiment with paint and express themselves in new and creative ways.

Skills

Visual

Creativity

Two Glass Plates 4 U 2 Paint
(Creativity for Kids)

Children can create and display unique decorative plates that they can actually use for their snacks, give as gifts or proudly exhibit. As the child paints her original design, its message and artistic composition reveals her attitudes, interests and values. The creative process is enriched when she produces something of significance that brings her recognition, confidence and self-esteem. This kit contains two glass plates, acrylic glaze paints and a paintbrush. The painted plate can solidify or bake in the oven to insure a protected permanent coating. Creating a one-of-a-kind decorative craft is a fulfilling activity, particularly because open-ended creativity and originality is fostered.

Creativity

S Motor

Skills

Poupette Sewing Set
(Corolle)

Especially made for small hands to manipulate with success, this classic doll is also a model for a first fashion design experience. As the child discovers how to dress a doll, she also learns how to make a dress *for* her doll. Creating doll clothing transforms early fantasy play into a rich, creative arts experience. Using Velcro and a beginning lacing and scissor set, the young child can string/sew a perfect dress for this small, articulated doll. Adding Velcro attachments and decoration adorn the dress and further increases the young child's individual, creative statement. In addition, eye-hand coordination and dexterity are strengthened.

My Origami & Kirigami Kit
(Alex)

The ancient Japanese art of Origami and Kirigami provides numerous folding and measuring activities while refining dexterity, small motor and perceptual skills. Although paper art can be a complex endeavor, this set and its projects and supplies are designed for young children's still emerging motor skills. This kit comes complete with multi-colored origami paper, other decorative papers, glue, child-friendly scissors, colored pens and stickers. The instructions are simple and clear to follow, and examples help children visualize finished products. While exploring the art forms of other lands, children gain new insight and tolerance and an increased understanding of other cultures as well as their own.

Potholders and Other Loopy Projects
(Klutz)

This classic weaving loom and cotton-blend loops are packaged with step-by-step instructions to help youngsters gain the satisfaction of completing a task independently, as well as developing crafts they can admire, share and use. While youngsters weave potholders, picture frames, purses and other simple articles, they bolster their attention spans, perceptual-motor skills and dexterity. Weaving techniques inspire youngsters to learn a pattern and duplicate that pattern while staying on task. These projects hone the young artist's basic sequencing skills and provide a fundamental and broad foundation for later, more challenging arts and crafts endeavors.

Hoberman Sphere
(Hoberman Designs)

Researchers have found that novelty and inventiveness are integral components of the creative arts process and that all children benefit from exposure to this process. This multi-sided "sphere" stimulates children's thinking and imaginative concept development. As a moving sculpture, it can be compressed and then opened back into its original shape. Since originality is an important fuel for creativity and passion for life, play with this product can be a stimulating and challenging experience that encourages children's resourcefulness, original thinking and inspiration.

Denim Rocks Fashion Designer Kit
(Malibu Toys)

This innovative fashion kit transforms children into fashion designers, and everyday denim clothing into works of wearable art. With creativity and some glue, denim jeans, shirts and accessories can be decorated with a child's own, original one-of-a-kind design using fabric accents, appliqués, sequins, ribbon, trim and fringe. The kit includes directions for sewing, and other projects with soft goods that can be customized to fit the individual child's personal tastes and promote her own creative expression. Wearable arts and crafts projects are fun and an excellent vehicle for creative expression.

MIRROR-ACULOUS Art Activities Kit
(OOZ & OZ)

This innovative "optical drawing" kit contains "mirror-tracing" activities for children to complete, draw and color. By using a rounded mirror and reflection tracing technique, children can decode what first looks like a distorted picture to the naked eye. Similar to what a mirror in a fun house might reveal, a cylinder-shaped mirror is at the basis of every colorful creation. This unique and challenging activity, called "anamorphosis," comes with a series of computer "morphed" drawings, a rounded mirror and crayons.

Woodkins
(Pamela Drake, Inc.)

Using wooden "dressable" dolls as models, young designers can create dozens of classic and contemporary fashion designs, complete with an array of fabrics, accessories and trims. These wooden sandwich-board doll puzzles fit tightly together to hold fabrics, ribbon and other specially selected fashion details in place. Cut-outs outline the shape of the clothing so young designers can drape the fabric over these manikins. Children demonstrate originality and ingenuity as they select and combine materials to produce various looks and costumes. Creativity is enhanced as play value provides numerous opportunities for design and personal fashion expressions.

Chapter 10: Toys For Children Who Build: Construction Toys

Creative play enhances learning and promotes feelings of confidence and competence. Through experimentation with open-ended building, children can discover, create, innovate and communicate. And, during the process of "trial and error" learning, children begin to better understand the world around them. Building toys can motivate individual and shared play and provide experiences for the development of numerous skills.

Construction toys stimulate discovery, problem solving and task completion strategies. As youngsters engage in the design and construction of building projects, they increase their visual and spatial awareness and refine their manual dexterity. The relationship of construction play to school achievement has long interested educators because of the close ties between perceptual abilities and academic achievement. Researchers have also found positive links between model building and spontaneous learning, with illustrations of this in almost every area of a child's visual-motor performance.

Also of importance to the growth and development of youngsters is the participation in symbolic and fantasy play that construction toys present. While building a bird feeder, space station, robot or skyscraper, the child injects her own symbolic representation into her play. A building becomes a backdrop for sorting reality from "make believe" and for learning future rules and roles.

The selection of appropriate construction toys should match the level of eye-hand coordination, dexterity, perceptual and intellectual abilities of the child. A product that is poorly made or too difficult for the child to manipulate will produce greater frustration than satisfaction. Similarly, one that is too simple or repetitive may not provide adequate motivation or challenge for the enthusiastic young builder. Among those construction toys recommended for school aged children are:

Mega Bloks
(Ritvik)

Oversized plastic pegged blocks are easy for preschoolers to take apart, fit together, and build upon. As blocks are combined, children develop and refine their eye-hand coordination, small motor skills and manual dexterity. Numerous opportunities for discovering spatial relationships and imaginative thought are provided. In addition, strategies for large-scale construction challenge a child's balance, visual perception and creativity. Wheels and angled pieces can be added to the structures for increased flexibility and movement. And, because of the large size of these blocks, young builders can make impressive constructions with a minimum number of pieces.

Ello
(Mattel)

This product combines the elements of building with those of design and story telling. Unique shapes, patterns and colors allow children to make unusual constructions including jewelry, wearable art, role-playing characters and modern structures. Unlike conventional building toys, small and large-scale decorative accessory items can be created with ovals, triangles, flowers and other organic shapes. Figurines, platforms and bridges can easily be built for fantasy performances. Themed sets such as underwater, jungle and fairyland fantasy are available in non-traditional color schemes of soft pastel colors.

Erector
(Brio)

This nuts and bolts construction system has been updated to emphasize new sophisticated moving parts, story themes and even 6V motors. However, Erector Sets are still traditional construction toys and true to their original hands-on manipulative building materials and style. Children develop skills while manipulating tools and working with various construction elements. Erector's versatile plastic chassis encourages coordination and participation in building. Children also gain experience in following step-by-step building plans and transforming those directions into actual tasks.

Gears! Gears! Gears! Building Set
(Learning Resources)

Initiating and observing change in the movement of interlocking gears provides a fascinating, yet simple illustration of the principle of cause and effect. Children are interested in learning about gears and how things work, and are curious about how the movement of one gear interacts with the movement of another. With the turn of a hand, a child can begin a chain reaction that will captivate her attention. Stackable gears and simple snap-together bases and connectors provide endless building possibilities. This product also includes pillars and cranks to encourage exploration and experimentation.

Capsela
(Educational Insights)

Transparent, interlocking capsules snuggly fit together and let young builders discover how gears, electrical circuits, motion and wheels interact to produce energy. "Hands on" visible building experiences engage youngsters and enhance learning through observation. These unique modules have working parts and fascinating high tech designs. Imaginative building is stimulated as children are exposed to the inner workings of gears and electricity, not usually visible in most motors or building sets. Children find the stark visibility of cause and effect relationships and scientific principles playing out right in front of their eyes to be thought provoking and exciting.

Ultimate NBA Arena
(Lego)

While constructing a miniature world of fantasy, children improve small motor coordination, concepts of balance in building, creative and imaginative thought and following directions. The basic components of the Lego system are Lego bricks, which are durable studded pieces of plastic that easily and securely combine with one another. These brightly colored bricks are the versatile cornerstone of a limitless number of building projects and possible constructions. One innovative building project features collectible superstar mini-figures that can actually shoot baskets. The set also contains everything necessary for constructing an authentic professional basketball arena.

Master Building Block System
(T.C. Timber)

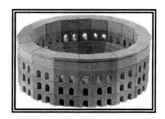

Domes and arches are just several of the many different shaped blocks that comprise this traditional building system. Natural wood blocks are favorites and grow along with children and families. When young builders share blocks and have a common goal, important socialization behaviors and attitudes can be established. During group or independent play, block play boosts visual discrimination skills and perceptual abilities while challenging children's ingenuity and planning and organizational talents. It is important to keep in mind, however, that play should be evaluated by the quality of each child's participation and learning, not the symbolic or elaborate outcome of a particular project.

Screamin' Serpent
(KNEX)

Color-coded rod and connector systems are combined into unique construction designs while children reinforce their eye-hand coordination and visual planning skills. "Hands on" building experiences engage youngsters and enhance learning through observation, reasoning, and balance. This product stimulates imaginative construction and reinforces perceptual motor skills. Children construct a "steel" style roller coaster that is over 6 1/2 feet long. A motor pulls the roller coaster cars up the incline track and "roller coaster" sound effects are included. A project such as this can become an individual or group-learning lab for discovering special relationships and developing innovative constructions.

Rok Works Start Set
(Rokenbok)

The Rok Works Start Set is a snap-together modular construction toy that combines open-ended model building with radio-controlled capabilities. The basic component of the Rokenbok system are "block and beam" elements that enable the young builder to challenge her creative building and problem-solving skills by creating construction sites with ramps, buildings, roadways, chutes and conveyors. Each set contains a radio controlled construction vehicle to move "building items" and to scoop up and haul the play cargo. A decoder is also provided for navigation of forklifts, dump trucks and other vehicles as they assist the child in the operation of her own model construction site.

ATOLLO
(ATTOLO)

This flexible construction system allows children to build "in the round" and offers the innovative product distinction of being flexible and bendable. In addition to building rigid structures, spheres, domes and even rounded animals can be created. Young builders will also quickly discover that this product can be integrated with other construction toys to extend the play value of all. A unique hinge and socket component allow flexible joints to bridge other brands of building sets so that compatible building elements can be combined. Learning is enhanced through motivating and successful building experiences, and children will find that almost any object or design can be replicated utilizing these pieces.

XI

Chapter 11: Toys For Children Who Travel

Any parent who has ever heard a resounding, "Are we there yet?" echo from the back seat of their car, knows that travel with kids can be challenging. But, as our society becomes more mobile, toys that can adapt to short and long excursions are increasingly in demand. Many children find transit uncomfortable, restrictive and confusing. From school carpools to cross country trips, travel rarely conforms to children's interests or limited attention spans. The right travel toys can reduce travel stress and make "getting there" a more pleasant and worthwhile experience.

Whether it's a boat cruise, car tour, bus trip, journey by train or plane ride, appropriate toys can be excellent travel companions for children. Several of the products recommended in this chapter were designed for use during travel. Others were selected simply because they are good toys that happen to travel well. While entertaining bored and restless young travelers, compact playthings that are simple to operate and contain few, if any, detachable or small loose pieces usually work best.

Not all aspects of transportation are burdensome, as exposure to new people and places can enrich a child's life and broaden her experience. In addition to keeping children occupied and comfortable, a mixture of activities that involve and distract them will keep even the youngest traveler engaged and relaxed.

Since travel often means unfamiliar surroundings, a special doll or favored plaything can be a bridge between home and the new environment and help a child to feel safe and secure. When a child feels lonely or is faced with an unknown setting, a familiar toy can be a welcomed friend. Children will benefit from keeping busy during travel and the "right" toys for their travels include:

Scrabble Express Electronic Hand Held Game
(Milton Bradley)

This is a take-everywhere version of the classic, challenging crossword game. It features a searchable dictionary, built-in scorekeeper and letter shuffler. This electronic, self-contained unit does away with the need for dozens of small wooden letter tiles and has no loose parts that are easily lost. It is an activity that encourages flexible thinking and visual memory, while accommodating children at various levels of vocabulary and word knowledge. During the play process, children build language skills, word recognition methods and strategic thinking strategies. Young Scrabble players are challenged by the deductive reasoning required to transform groups of letters into high scoring words.

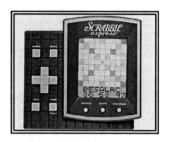

Etch-A-Sketch
(Ohio Art)

This hand-held draw and dial toy is great for developing perceptual motor skills, eye-hand coordination and creativity. Each time a child creates a new picture, she does so without using crayons, a pencil or even paper. This quiet activity allows children to "draw" in vertical and horizontal directions, using a stylus to create original artwork and geometric designs. An excellent lap toy with no loose parts, children can increase their concentration abilities and "task persistence" while they play. Vinyl game sheets that cling to the screen bring additional dimension and play value to the product.

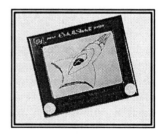

103

Crayola Lap Desk
(Crayola)

This portable, child-sized lap desk is great for travel and for creating artwork anywhere. It has a detachable, washable fleece cushion for secure lap placement which doubles as a pillow for comfortable naps while in transit. A variety of art materials and templates make creative projects exciting and easily adjustable to the individual child's interests and abilities. While occupied with appropriate art projects, children stay engaged and attentive during long periods of travel. And, access to art materials encourages even the youngest travelers to keep visual records of their travel experiences and record those memories in a meaningful way.

Adventure Traveling Suitcase
(Hasbro Preschool)

This rolling suitcase filled with role-playing sun glasses, phone, computer screen and keyboard, meal tray and luggage tags helps the young child act out and understand what actually happens during travel. And, it allows her to act "just like" her parents as she rehearses the roles of adulthood. Props that help a child imagine and replicate real experiences as well as encounters with unfamiliar "grown up" activities are useful in dealing with the many emotions of travel. These feelings that can range from restlessness and boredom to excitement and anxiety are as much a focus of a child's vacation experiences as visiting relatives or seeing new places.

Lamaze Back Seat Fun Center
(Learning Curve)

A flexible bar with mirrors, balls and rattles make this durable stroller accessory and back seat car toy an exciting visual and auditory environment for baby. This moving play center, with its numerous attached toys and activities, will occupy baby's travel time and teach and entertain even the youngest passenger. Toys hang for easy grasp and are age-appropriate and especially geared for specific developmental level and ability. Objects for mouthing, reaching and hand-to-hand exchange are included, engaging baby's attention and interest while encouraging independent activity.

Talk Time
(Wild Planet)

When a child is traveling away from home, waking up to mother's voice, big sister's morning song or grandpa saying "Time for breakfast!" can be most reassuring. Providing a linkage to family and all that is familiar brings focus and warmth to youngsters away from home. This unique alarm clock with a recorded voice message can help the first time camper or young traveler bring a sense of home and family with her -- even when she is away from home. A friendly and familiar voice can lift and comfort the anxious child.

Travel Magna Doodle
(Fisher- Price)

This familiar magnetic drawing product travels with ease. A pen-like stylus allows children to write and draw at any place and at anytime. Since no materials can spill or drop and balance is not an important factor, this is an excellent lap toy and back seat design studio. Children can write notes, play games and draw with the stylus and erase their work by simply moving a bar across the screen. Magnets of different shapes and sizes can also be used to create original patterns and images by pressing them across the drawing surface.

Lamaze Car Seat Activity Center
(Learning Curve)

Sitting in a car seat does not have to be a passive experience for the traveling baby. This activity center was especially designed to keep baby amused, engaged and seated during travel. The soft foam play center has various extensions and manipulative activities as well as a teething turtle attached. In addition to having fun, the trip can be a fun learning experience. A hippo that plays peek-a-boo reinforces the concept of object constancy and a giraffe that moves and makes music provides interactive, visual and auditory stimulation.

Turbo Twist Handheld Brain Quest
(LeapFrog)

This hand-held learning game automatically adjusts to a child's skill level and offers her academic encouragement. The child masters fact-based questions about school subjects, and then is ready to ask even more questions. Games are blends of history, science, English and geography course work and content is reinforced by a musical beat. Additional content categories and subjects can be downloaded from the Internet for extended play value. The child is rewarded with each correct answer and encouraged to try again when an incorrect answer is selected.

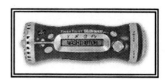

GeoSafari Talking Globe Traveler
(Educational Insights)

When the child is traveling in the world, it's a perfect opportunity to learn *about* the world. Digital speech, lights, and sounds quiz children with over 5,000 fascinating questions about countries and cultures with this compact electronic geography game. The travel unit features "talking" questions and answers that engage the young traveler in a plane, train or car. In addition to making the subject of geography fun, this stimulating learning game will allow the child to play independently and inspire her to learn about the larger world.

Hand-Held Boggle
(Milton Bradley)

Young players score points by creating as
many unique three- and four- letter words as
possible within a three-minute play period.
This hand-held electronic game holds a
child's attention and provides an action-
oriented and enthusiastic experience for the
traveling youngster. Working within a
framework of individual letter cues, children
add and combine letters to create simple
words. In the process of word building, the
child enlarges her vocabulary and develops
important perceptual and problem-solving
skills. Boggle can be played individually -
against the "clock" - or with others. This fast
moving, electronic game reinforces focus
and concentration and helps to pass the time
on a long car ride or airplane flight.

XII

Chapter 12: Toys for Children with Special Needs

All children are exceptional, with unique learning styles and distinctive talents. However, children who have special needs, such as physical, emotional, visual or hearing challenges, or cognitive difficulties including mental retardation and learning differences, can greatly benefit from toys that address their individual educational goals. They will be well served by toys that are adapted to challenge their abilities and reflect their potential. Appropriate toys can help children to develop important skills and areas of social and emotional competence. Additionally, they provide enjoyable experiences that foster confidence and self-esteem.

Through play, the child with special needs builds many competencies that will ultimately enable her to participate more fully in mainstreamed school experiences, play opportunities and home settings. The normalization of play allows all children to interact and participate, to the greatest extent possible, with siblings and peers.

For the child who is recuperating from an illness or temporarily indisposed, the "right" toys can soften a hospital environment and provide a comfortable link between the home, school and professional services. And, for all children, play can provide a foundation for learning, socialization, communication and friendship.

The Lekotek Center, a national organization that advocates the use of toys, play and family interaction in the education of children with disabilities, recommends the following considerations be raised when selecting toys for children with special needs:

Multisensory appeal: Does the toy respond with lights, sounds, or other movement? Does it have bright colors, a scent or texture?

Method of activation: Will the toy provide a challenge to the child without frustration? What force is required to activate the toy?

Where the toy will be used: Can the toy be used in a variety of positions such as side lying or on a wheelchair tray?

Opportunities for success: Can play be flexible and open-ended with no definite right or wrong way? Is it adaptable to the child's individual style, ability and pace?

Current popularity: Is it a toy most children know and want? Does it tie-in with other popular themes from television, movies or books?

Self-expression: Does the toy allow for creativity, uniqueness, and decision-making? Will it give the child experience with a variety of media?

Adjustability: Does it have adjustable height, sound volume, speed and level of difficulty?

Child's individual characteristics: Does the toy provide activities that reflect the child's developmental and chronological ages? Does it reflect the child's interests?

Safety and durability: Is the toy sized appropriately? Can it be washed and cleaned?

<u>Potential for interaction</u>: Will the child be an active participant during use? Will the toy encourage socialization with others?

Most parents and educators of children with learning, physical and sensory challenges agree that children with disabilities do not, necessarily, require "special education" toys or playthings with elaborate modifications and adaptive designs. But, like all children, youngsters with special needs can - and do - benefit from exposure to toys specifically chosen to reflect their unique learning and play needs.

Toys for the Visually Challenged Child:

Through play that is rich in sensory stimulation and feedback, the child with limited visual ability can sharpen her channels of learning and communication. Since many partially sighted and blind children rely primarily on sound and touch for information about the world, toys that provide motivating auditory and tactile experiences can be important teaching tools. While interacting with these playthings, opportunities for refining sensory and visual discrimination abilities as well as other cognitive and perceptual-motor skills are provided. A wide range of sensory input stimulates a child's curiosity in the world and helps to promote her self-esteem and confidence. Among those toys recommended for children with visual impairments are:

Tactile Bars
(Guidecraft)

Tactile skills are reinforced as the visually limited child compares and contrasts a row of various, interesting textures. This wooden board is comprised of nine distinct textured components ranging from rough to smooth and including such discreet sensations and materials as metal, sandpaper and carpet. Components slide on and off a bar for matching activities and for sequencing and memory coaching. By sharpening perceptual competencies and developing perceptual strengths, many youngsters can compensate for the more limited information they gain through exclusively visual channels.

Tic-Tock Answer Clock
(TOMY)

Like all abstract concepts, measuring time becomes a more concrete and understandable activity with appropriate learning tools that reinforce practical life-skills and abilities. Through oversized knobs, raised numbers and large clock hands, this "owl-themed" clock helps children learn to tell time and become familiar with hours and minutes. For youngsters with limited vision, in particular, this toy fosters perceptual awareness and introduces them to digital and analog time-telling techniques. In addition to explaining concepts like "before and after," parents can refer to this friendly timepiece throughout the day.

Shake 'N Carnival
(Shelcore)

Happy carnival music reinforces play with toys that include a carnival cage, ride and parade cannon. Sounds reinforce learning as this extension of listening skills is coupled with the use of visual and tactile reinforcement. Sound, characters and actions come together to create important developmental learning competencies in low vision and blind children. In addition to providing an opportunity to sharpen thinking and learning, cause and effect relationships and small motor skills, the ability to understand and respond to auditory cues should be practiced and supported. Tactile discrimination between shapes should also be reinforced to build touch as an effective learning channel for these youngsters.

Phonics from A to Z
(VTech)

An interactive "talking" language toy, this phonics keyboard entertains as it teaches. Children experience the sound and feel of alphabet letters in addition to being exposed to the feel of the Braille alphabet. Based on a series of raised dots, this product introduces the Braille alphabet and enables visually challenged children to practice the reading of Braille and the sounds of phonics. Within this framework, object identification and spelling are reinforced, and both sighted and visually challenged children gain an understanding of the Braille alphabet. This use of technologically enhanced products enables all children to explore alternative learning methods with mainstream educational toys.

Skwish Classic
(Manhattan Toy)

Children are fascinated to hold and explore the construction of this three-dimensional puzzle. While inspecting the linkages of the wooden dowels and beads, children with visual and perceptual limitations can discover how separate parts connect and interconnect to better understand building strategies. Tactile manipulation promotes the growth of eye-hand coordination as well as important dexterity skills. While holding a developmental learning toy or rattle, youngsters can feel the balance and construction of an object and examine it from various perspectives. In addition to sharpening tactile awareness, play with this sphere stimulates mathematical reasoning and can assist in problem solving skills.

Toys for the Hearing Challenged Child:

The categories of hearing impairments and the severity of loss associated with them vary greatly. However, toys best suited for children with all levels of hearing difficulties are those that encourage the development of multi-sensory learning channels and foster language and communication. By strengthening all of the senses, dependence on a single sound cue is diminished. The right playthings, therefore, should stimulate speech and "total communication" while motivating each child to interact with the environment to the fullest extent possible. Since deaf children live in a hearing world, toys with loud noises and vibrations can be utilized to help the hearing-impaired child make important distinctions between sounds. With these mainstreamed toys, deaf and hard of hearing youngsters play with their hearing peers and learn how to best understand the reactions of others to them. Among those toys recommended for children with hearing impairments are:

Electronic Hand-held Simon
(Milton Bradley)

Numerous cognitive challenges are provided by fast-moving, electronic games where players must repeat a sequence or pattern that gets progressively longer and faster. Often there are only sound cues to guide players and to establish the play pattern and relationships. This toy, however, features four different colored lenses that light up as the sequence is presented. This continuing sequence of flashing lights builds on the visual learning abilities and the visual-perceptual strengths of children with hearing impairments. While sharing this game with normal hearing siblings or peers, a positive play experience in a mainstream setting can occur.

Kids' Kit
(Magnetic Poetry)

A focus on language-based activities and play with visual language cues are highly recommended for children with hearing difficulties. These word and phrase magnets offer endless possibilities for creating sentences, short stories and poetry or simply playing with words and exploring language. Attention to words and language as a component of play for hearing impaired children will reinforce total communication and encourage speech. Keeping a hearing impaired child's words, poems or other original writing on display around the refrigerator or on another magnetic surface confirms her achievements and celebrates her abilities.

Little People Fun Sounds Garage
(Fisher-Price)

Since many children with hearing loss have residual hearing ability, toys that emit specific sounds may be appropriate for encouraging auditory discrimination and listening skills. One such toy with distinctive sounds and vibrations is the Little People Fun Sounds Garage. Children can pretend to fill up toy cars with gas, go through the car wash, and even have car repairs done. Each action on one of the garage's three levels of ramps, elevators, and car lifts produces a corresponding sound including a gas pump that rings, horns that honk and even tools that make realistic sounds. And, since background noises can be screened out in an indoor play setting, the linkage of specific sounds to objects can be clear and particularly helpful to children with mild or moderate hearing loss.

Plan Toys Geometric Sorting Board
(BRIO)

This classic sorting board has four distinct shapes to promote visual discrimination, perceptual learning and small motor development. Each shape has four colorful pieces for children to match to the correct shape and corresponding wood pegs. Young children with severe auditory disabilities are trained on visual and tactile materials for concept formation, information gathering and confidence building. This strong, visual foundation enables them to predict relationships, problem-solve and become keenly aware of visual cues present in the environment. Visual materials provide children who are deaf or severely hard-of-hearing with effective and positive feedback on their learning strategies and problem solving abilities.

118

Toys for the Physically Challenged Child:

Through exploratory movement, investigation and interaction, the young child learns about herself and the world in which she lives. For the youngster whose physical mobility is impaired or significantly delayed, these important early learning opportunities are limited and often frustrating. Appropriate toys can normalize play experiences and motivate interaction with other youngsters and with the environment. Toys can be used to enhance motor learning and reinforce skill development. Feelings of adequacy and confidence emerge through successful participation in play. During muscular activity, specific motor disabilities are augmented and improved, including impairments of balance, coordination and involuntary movement. Toys that meet the special needs of children with physical disabilities include:

Miss Weather Colorforms Stick-Ons
(Colorforms)

A traditional activity kit with reusable stickers and a smooth board invites children to dress and decorate pictures without the frustration of cutting, pasting or folding. A child challenged by cerebral palsy, involuntary movement or limited upper body strength, can provide a light contact between the plastic Colorforms and the background board illustration that will result in the successful "sticking" of the form to the board. Various background illustrations are available to capture the child's interest and motivate her interaction. Dressing Colorform dolls, for example, is fun and develops eye-hand coordination, refines small motor skills and teaches about appropriate clothing for the weather.

Mozart Magic Cube
(Munchkin)

Children with physical limitations should be able to activate and interact with their toys, independently. This innovative musical cube plays realistic musical sounds that reinforce participation in play. Each push of a large colorful button activates the sound of an individual musical instrument or that of an entire orchestra. This interaction encourages cause and effect learning and helps the child to feel empowered. Confidence is built as the pressure of a child's own hand on the button produces the musical notes of a harp, French horn, piano, flute or violin. And, for the child with physical disabilities, a rubber, non-slide bottom stabilizes the toy during play.

Shape Bean Bags
(Learning Resources)

Throwing and catching are complex physical-motor tasks and often a source of frustration to the child with physical coordination problems. Large soft beanbags, however, can provide tactile assistance in the development of perceptual-motor skills and eye-hand coordination. The refinement of these skills and corresponding physical movement help the child with physical challenges experience greater success in physical activities and sports. By simplifying the throw and catch activity, the quality of the disabled child's interaction and play becomes more pleasurable and fun. In addition, beanbags of various shapes reinforce the child's understanding of triangle, circle, square and rectangle in a concrete and understandable way.

Little Smart Baby Hoops
(VTech)

This sports-themed "fit and drop" task, develops eye-hand coordination, visual and physical alignment and concentration. Children with physical challenges can develop and refine their motor accuracy while playing "mini-basketball". Each time the ball is thrown through a hoop, the "score" and a "hooray" are flashed on a light-up screen. Children with physical disabilities are reinforced for normalized play and have fun while practicing their aim, directionality and throwing skills. In addition, they experience competitive athletic "victory" and self-confidence as musical tunes and sound effects herald their winning baskets and stimulate their motor-learning successes.

Lamaze Musical Octotunes
(Learning Curve)

When a youngster reaches out and grabs one of the eight legs of this colorful, plush musical animal, she is greeted by different sounds and notes and will be encouraged to continue reaching, grasping and playing. This toy provides an auditory reward each time one of the musical legs is pressed. Its high-contrast colors and sound effects encourage examination and physical interaction. For children with poor muscle tone and limited hand strength or whose disability requires increased exercise of the arms and hands, movement inspired by music motivates the manipulation of objects during play. A variety of textures for grip and grasp, and dexterity are provided to enhance exploration.

122

Toys for the Learning Disabled Child:

Children with learning disabilities often show a discrepancy between their learning potential and actual school performance. Many LD youngsters experience frustration in learning and problems in social and recreational situations as well. Therefore, in selecting toys for youngsters with cognitive, emotional, or attention difficulties, priority should be given to playthings that inspire success and confidence building rather than possible feelings of disappointment or inadequacy. Toys for children with learning differences should address particular learning needs and assist in the development of organizational, perceptual, memory and social skills. Playthings should focus on specific behavioral and learning competencies as well as opportunities for the child to experience the successful completion of a task. Some toys that meet the special needs of children with learning disabilities include:

Radio DJ Studio
(Wild Planet)

Socialization skills and expressive language competencies are developed as the child with learning difficulties experiences the fun of being a disk jockey at her own radio station. Auditory discrimination is reinforced as laughter, cheering, a drum roll and buzzer enhance play with dramatic sound effects. A soundboard, complete with fade-in controls, allows the child to mix her voice with music or make karaoke-style recordings. When the "On Air" light goes on, it signals that it is time to speak into the microphone and begin the show in the "studio".

Lacing and Tracing Custom Set
(Lauri)

Reading disorders are often linked to specific learning delays and poor visual-perceptual skills. In a reading-readiness setting, this may translate into difficulties identifying objects and shapes and distinguishing between various letters. Similarly, the small-motor and eye-hand coordination problems of the learning-challenged child may first be apparent in areas like coloring, copying and buttoning. These lacing shapes reinforce emerging finger flexibility and fine-motor coordination. While exposing youngsters to a variety of defined shapes for manipulation and lacing, agility and dexterity can be reinforced.

Baby Annabell
(Zapf)

Play props can be helpful as the young child prepares for the arrival of a new baby brother or sister. Of special assistance is a baby doll that can take some of the mystery away from the explanation process and ease the long wait for the new birth. In addition to rehearsing actual nurturing and kindness behaviors, interacting with this sound and motion-sensitive doll can give the soon-to-be sibling confidence as well as experience. Reacting to sound and touch, this doll is able to stop crying when her tummy is rubbed and will burp while being lifted.

Math Lab
(VTech)

This product's unique, three-dimensional system of teaching math is particularly effective with LD children. Exposure to arithmetic involves active participation as children push a lever to "add," or twist a knob, clockwise, to increase number sequences. Conversely, pulling a lever subtracts or "takes away" and a counter-clockwise rotation of the knob decreases numbers. Concrete representations of abstract math concepts are valuable teaching tools for all children. Products that teach math concepts through fun and hands-on methods are particularly beneficial for the learning disabled. Regardless of the learning style, we know that LD children learn best by "doing."

Paired Up Junior
(Games For All Reasons)

Matching and sorting activities help to develop visual recognition skills and attention-focusing strategies. Creating groups of objects that are alike, different, or of a particular shape or color enables children to practice grouping and clustering techniques that they will continue to use throughout their lives. Matching items helps children to see items that go together and those that connect with one another. This game encourages problem-solving skills and can include matching and pairing exercises and other non-competitive learning activities.

Toys for the Mentally Challenged Child:

Mental retardation is an intellectual disability characterized by below-average mental functioning and difficulties in social and daily living skills. The MR child is challenged in intellectual functioning and may have problems understanding abstract ideas and concepts. Playthings for children with retarded mental development should reflect their limitations, but focus on their strengths and abilities. Toys for these children should be motivating and challenging, but not overly complex, frustrating, or above the MR child's level of understanding. The right toys should offer parents and teachers of children with retarded mental development the opportunity to build on the concrete and manipulative strengths that the child has already developed. Toys should enhance the individual child's ability to organize and process information while reinforcing her areas of accomplishment and success. Toys that meet the special needs of intellectually challenged children include:

Be A Star Ballerina
(Silver Dolphin Books)

Performance as role-playing can spark a child's imagination and build confidence and self esteem. Imaginative tools that enhance the fantasy world for a child can help her to form a significant pretend environment. This product includes all the props and sounds necessary for the creation of a magical, creative world of music and dance. A CD contains the music from the Nutcracker and a tiara, tickets and posters help reinforce the fantasy. As a ballerina, the young girl can act out scenarios and play many roles. In addition to fostering creative expression, this product challenges listening and concentration abilities and stimulates physical expression and pride.

Fun With Your Dog!
(Scientific Explorer)

Children's love for animals – and, in particular, for their own pet -- is incorporated into this teaching and play science kit for training and building responsible animal-care behaviors. In the same way that children enjoy playing doctor and taking care of dolls and stuffed animals, youngsters will enjoy role-play veterinarian and, in the process, attend to their own pets. The young child can learn all about their pet's personality as well as the foods pets really like. While studying her dog's behavior and ability to navigate in the world, the youngster learns what to look for in a happy animal's behavior. The process is educational, and a great way to promote socialization, empathy and responsibility.

A to Z Links
(The First Years)

This linked alphabet chain can enhance the development of tactile and sensory channels and reinforce alphabet learning. While holding and linking letters together, the child with developmental learning challenges can touch, compare and recognize the unique and distinct shape of each letter in the alphabet. Utilizing a sensory approach, this activity fosters visual awareness as well as tactile exploration. Open-ended activities, including the manipulation of an alphabet chain such as this, are important strategies in the reinforcement of abstract concepts and concrete learning experiences. These touch and hold activities encourage continued play, interest in the alphabet and tactile discovery.

Puppets
(Folkmanis)

Puppet play facilitates socialization, empathy and emotional growth. It is also a wonderful medium for speech and language development and vocabulary building. Puppet play can be achieved individually or within groups as various play parts can be combined to create an endless number of puppet characters and situations. Language -rich activities allow children to act out various situations and can be heightened by large and imaginative puppets such as these. In addition to social interaction and language reinforcement, motor abilities, including perceptual skills and eye-hand coordination are also enhanced.

129

Bitty Twins
(Pleasant Company)

Through interaction with a soft-bodied doll, the mentally retarded child can communicate caring, practice language skills, learn responsible behaviors and rehearse social interactions. In addition to providing a platform for socialization and learning, a special doll can ease separations such as bedtime or other transitions. Dolls can act as an important bridge between the security of home and transitions to school, doctors' offices and even new babysitters. Mental retardation includes social delays and challenges in establishing age-appropriate relationships. These baby twin dolls can provide play vehicles and stimulate socialization experiences for both girls and boys.

Alphabet Blocks
(Schylling)

Traditional wooden blocks featuring embossed letters and numbers gently reinforce academic concepts while children experiment with balance, block building and spatial relationships. Engaging and entertaining, blocks provide intellectually challenged children with opportunities for interacting with others or solitary play. Children with limited intellectual ability may depend on several different modalities for learning about language and math. Used as an important pre-school readiness tool, these blocks can emphasize letter and number recognition. Whether a child is solving problems that evolve naturally during play or creating a new building scenario, the educational value of blocks is indisputable.

130

Uncover a Race Car
(Silver Dolphin Books)

This unique combination of reading activity and layered "investigation" makes this set perfectly suited for the child who needs additional time in discovering how things work. Combining the best elements of a fascinating book, the popular subject of racecars and a three-dimensional replica of a car, the child can "uncover" the mysteries of what makes the racecar work. Children will relish the opportunity to explore the dynamics of racing and, literally, get underneath the hood of the car and explore the workings of the engine. Through "peeling away" the book's eight layers, the model of a racecar is uncovered and the child with special needs can focus on many interesting racecar facts and pictures.

Toys for the Intellectually Gifted Child:

Gifted children often demonstrate the potential for exceptional academic performance, creativity and leadership. Their extreme curiosity and unique concentration abilities may enable them to readily comprehend complex relationships. Children with superior intelligence often exhibit creativity and originality in their approaches to solving problems as well as the capacity to learn quickly. The "right" toys for high-ability youngsters are those that enrich their learning environments and life experiences and present new opportunities for exploration and investigation. Playthings for children with superior intellectual abilities, as for all youngsters, should primarily be vehicles for fun that promote self-esteem and competence. However, toys for gifted children should additionally reflect their need for challenging developmental opportunities. Several products recommended for gifted and talented children are:

Junior Explorer Globe
(LeapFrog)

This interactive, talking globe teaches young children about the world in which they live. With the touch of a pointer, the curious youngster can listen to information, realistic sound effects and music from any particular region of the world. While learning the geography, landmarks, languages and animal groups associated with various parts of the world, she is better able to integrate this comprehensive view and draw meaningful conclusions from the information presented. This globe will challenge the gifted child to explore the many facets of science, geography and world cultures in a way that is relevant to her age, level of experience and interests.

Observer 60
(Orion)

Every aspiring young scientist has yearned for a powerful telescope or large-aperture refractor that can produce unobstructed, crystal clear images of far off worlds. This amazing telescope can provide high ability children who have strong interests and aptitude in the sciences with an opportunity to study planets and stars, uninhibited by poor visibility. Children will be challenged and excited to view the lunar landscape in vivid detail or distinguish the rings of Saturn. The curiosity and concentration of gifted children enable them to readily comprehend and appreciate an opportunity for high-powered exploration of our solar system.

Theatre Set
(LEGO)

Children love to build theatrical "sets" and then present plays with miniature characters. This set combines both building and performance activities. It challenges children of high ability to manipulate detailed play figures and props and incorporate them into intricate story patterns. Building a theatre is an excellent backdrop for refining small motor skills and fantasy role-playing. And, it is a stimulating vehicle for expanding imaginative and language-rich interactions between children. Creative building of theatrical structures and of stories will entertain and educate high ability children with opportunities for imaginative and open-ended play.

Rush Hour
(Binary Arts)

Gifted children often exhibit highly effective and unique methods for solving problems. This game, a variation on the traditional sliding-block puzzle, challenges sequential-thinking skills and stimulates strategic thinking. The goal of this game is to move through a crowded maze – a traffic jam – and free up spaces on a grid as the player evaluates potential solutions. This process requires working through complex problems and seeking strategic answers. Opportunities for successful problem solving reinforce the gifted child's self-esteem and enthusiasm for learning. And, since there is no single, correct solution, youngsters are inspired to think "out of the box" and in new and innovative ways.

Reading Rods Phonics Activity Sets
(Learning Resources)

From phonetic awareness to word and sentence building, these interlocking blocks are a unique approach to language arts and to sharpening reading skills. Children can link letters to make words and combine words to build sentences. Consonant blends, vowels, punctuation and parts of speech are among the many lessons within this comprehensive literacy kit. Children can set their own learning pace and progress and develop word rods that range from very simple to exceedingly complex. Gifted children will discover many new words and concepts and will be challenged by the open-ended nature of the words and the construction.

iQuest Handheld
(Leap Frog)

Study the spelling words and take the quiz. And not just any spelling words or quiz – *your* current class spelling words and quiz! This handheld devise allows students to stay on top of their schoolwork even while they are out of school. Curriculum, based on the actual textbooks used in the child's classroom, is transformed into outlines and activities for learning. Regardless if a child is traveling, absent or late for school, she can keep up with her academic work. Additional cartridges with pre-programmed outlines, quizzes and other materials are available at retail and also through an internet subscription service. This innovative tool keeps students "on task," functioning as an address book, calendar, electronic note pad and dictionary.

Toys for the Convalescent Child:

During the period of recovery and convalescence, play can provide a link between the inactivity and isolation of an illness and the normalcy of childhood. Toys can help a young patient conquer the isolation and boredom of a hospital stay or extended period of bed rest. In general, toys for the recovering child should be geared to lower amounts of energy and physical activity as well as for shortened periods of attention. Play with appropriate toys can serve an important therapeutic function. It can also be a vehicle for expression of feelings and fears often associated with the infirmities of childhood. Importantly, toys can bring a dimension of fun and happiness into the life of a convalescing child. Some of the right toys for recovering children include:

Old Century Baseball
(Front Porch Classics)

This classic, wooden, old-fashioned pinball game does not require batteries or electricity! A mini-ballpark creates the setting for old-time baseball. This table or bed-top game is sturdy and utilizes a flipper bat on a spring. This product enables the recovering child to score base hits, doubles, triples as well as home runs. Since the day can be a long one for children who are home from school because of illness -- particularly during long convalescent periods - toys that are fun and skill-based can be therapeutic and curative. When visitors stop by several players can take turns as a scoreboard records the play-by-play on the field.

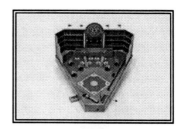

Sprout & Grow Window
(Educational Insights)

This transparent 'nature's window' allows children to plant seeds, care for living things and experience a sense of accomplishment as they watch their garden sprout and grow. For children who are hospitalized or at home recuperating from an illness, caring for this window garden is an important daily ritual and helps them to learn responsibility and gain a sense of self-confidence. Special potting soil nurtures bean, pea and other seedlings so growth is fast and reinforcing. Addressing the boredom that often accompanies convalescence or extended bed rest is challenging and the expectation and excitement of the change and growth of a garden may be just what the doctor ordered!

Icee Maker
(Spin Master)

When children are home recuperating, they will particularly enjoy using this frozen drinks icemaker. For some medical conditions, sucking on ice can bring comfort and hydration. An innovative "deep freeze" process allows children and their visitors to churn and carve ice without electricity or batteries. Salt, ice and water are cranked for approximately five minutes and, as a temperature transfer occurs, a crushed ice drink is easily produced. A food activity toy can be fun as an individual or shared activity and helps to pass the long hours of recuperation.

Precious Day Girls
(Gotz)

The doll as companion, nurturing friend and familiar plaything during a worrisome time remains an important theme in fantasy play. A doll can be a child's staunch supporter during periods of medical care and recovery, and steadfast ally throughout therapeutic treatment. Not only can a child fantasize that a doll "friend" is there for her, but that she is needed and the doll benefits from *her* love and attention. Easing transitions between home and hospital or school and doctor, this beautiful, realistic doll conveys feelings of security and familiarity when situations may be intimidating or when a child feels anxious or apprehensive.

Vehicle Designer Light Up Tracing Desk
(Crayola)

This unique laptop light-box makes tracing a comfortable bedside activity. The recovering youngster can choose from a large assortment of vehicle tracing shapes to create cars and other designs. Tracing pencils and paper are also included in this kit and can be stored right in the portable desk. Through involvement in creative projects and art activities, the recuperating child can stay focused on being productive and active. Artwork helps to maintain a sense of normalcy and can become a lifeline as well as a creative outlet for the inactive, convalescing child.

Traveling Flash Cards
(Munchkin)

Colorful word and number flash cards can be stimulating companions during long days of recuperation. This skill-building set includes graphic images of over 80 objects to challenge the child's letter, word, shape, and color recognition abilities. These innovative cards are secured like a flip chart with large rings on a textured and easy-to-hold handle. They can be used in bed or virtually anywhere and stay attached should they be dropped. As a reading and math-readiness tool, this card deck promotes vocabulary, identification and classification skills as well as increased confidence.

Van Gogh & Friends Art Game
(Birdcage Books)

Budding artists can "fish" for the paintings they like the most and, in the process, learn about famous artists and well known paintings. Based on the game of "Go Fish", thirty playing cards, decorated with the most famous paintings in the world, bring the fine arts into the hands of interested youngsters and into the realm of game-playing fun. A mixture of art, education and entertainment, children learn fascinating and little-known facts about art while fully engaged in the game which is sure to hold their attention.

NFL Super Bowl Electric Football
(Miggle Toys)

As the child recovers, her sports play may be limited to the tabletop or bedside. This traditional "vibrating top" electric football game allows the player to be both her team's star quarterback and coach, moving a 3-dimensional team down the field. Strategy involves setting up various formations and then letting the electric vibration system "spread" the players out on the field and moving toward the goal. The realistic, miniature football field comes with goal posts, first down marker and even a ten-yard chain. Successful play does not require precise agility or extreme physical strength.

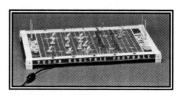

CLASSIC TOYS ... STILL ON THE MARKET!

The Toy Industry Association has compiled a list of our all-time favorite, classic toys, the year they were introduced and their current manufacturers:

1867-1929

1867 Parcheesi Game	Milton Bradley Co.
1900 Lionel Trains	Lionel LLC
1903 Crayola Crayons	Binney & Smith, Inc.
1904 Pit Game	Winning Moves Inc.
1905 Flinch Game	Winning Moves Inc.
1906 Rook Game	Parker Brothers
1906 Model T Ford	Strombecker Corp.
1913 Erector Sets	BRIO Corporation
1914 Tinkertoys	Playskool, Div. of Hasbro
1916 Lincoln Logs	K'NEX Industries, Inc.
1917 Wagon	Radio Flyer Inc.
1929 Yo-Yo	Duncan Toys Company

1930s

1930 LEGO Building Sets	LEGO Systems, Inc.
1932 Tripoley Game	Cadaco, Inc.
1934 Sorry Game	Parker Brothers
1938 View-Master 3-D	Fisher-Price, Div. of Mattel
1938 Head of the Class	Milton Bradley, Div. of Hasbro

1940s

1943 Chutes and Ladders	Milton Bradley Co.
1946 Tonka Trucks	Hasbro, Inc.
1946 Nylint Trucks	Nylint Corp.
1947 John Deere Tractor	Ertl Company, Inc.
1948 Cootie	Milton Bradley Co.
1948 Scrabble Game	Milton Bradley Co.
1949 Candy Land	Milton Bradley Co.
1949 Clue Parker Brothers,	Hasbro, Inc.

1950s

1950 Silly Putty	Binney & Smith, Inc.
1950 Wooly Willy	Smethport Specialty Company
1952 Mr. Potato Head	Playskool, Div. of Hasbro
1954 Jotto Game	Endless Games
1954 Matchbox Cars	Mattel, Inc.
1955 Play-Doh	Hasbro, Inc.

1956 Yahtzee Game	Milton Bradley Co.
1956 Original Ant Farm	Uncle Milton Industries, Inc.
1956 Ticklebee Game	Endless Games
1957 Careers Game	Pressman Toy Corp.
1958 Beat the ClockGame	Endless Games
1958 Concentration Game	Endless Games
1959 Barbie	Mattel, Inc.

1960s

1960 Aggravation Game	Milton Bradley Co.
1960 Kismet Game	Endless Games
1960 Etch-A-Sketch	Ohio Art Company
1960 BRIO Railway	BRIO Corporation
1960 Life	Milton Bradley Co.
1961 Stratego	Milton Bradley Co.
1962 Mille Bornes Card Game	Winning Moves Inc.
1963 G.I. Joe	Hasbro, Inc.
1963 Easy Bake Oven	Hasbro, Inc.
1964 Easy Ride'Ums Animals	Mary Meyer Corp.
1964 Rummikub	Pressman Toy Corp.
1964 Password Game	Endless Games
1964 Rat Fink Figures	Collectible, Inc.
1965 Trouble	Milton Bradley Co.
1965 Operation	Milton Bradley Co.
1966 Spirograph	Hasbro, Inc.
1966 Twister	Milton Bradley Co.

1966 Memory Game	Milton Bradley Co.
1967 Battleship	Milton Bradley Co.
1968 Hot Wheels Cars	Mattel, Inc.

1970s

1970 Marshall Brodien Cards	Cadaco, Inc.
1970 Nerf Balls	Hasbro, Inc.
1970 Bachmann Trains	Bachmann Industries, Inc.
1971 Mastermind Game	Pressman Toy Corp.
1972 Uno Card Game	Mattel, Inc.
1974 Connect Four	Milton Bradley Co.
1974 Waggie Lamb	Learning Curve International
1975 Othello	Pressman Toy Corp.
1978 Simon Electronic	Milton Bradley Co.
1978 Hungry Hungry Hippos	Milton Bradley Co.
1979 Rubik's Cube	OddzOn, Div. of Hasbro, Inc.

1980s

1982 Sequence Game	Jax Ltd., Inc.
1983 Cabbage Patch Kids	Mattel, Inc.
1983 Phase 10 Card Game	Fundex Games
1983 Trivial Pursuit	Hasbro, Inc.
1983 Read a Mat	Straight Edge, Inc.
1984 Transformers	Hasbro, Inc.
1984 Lee Middleton Dolls	Lee Middleton Original Dolls

1985 Wheel of Fortune	Mattel, Inc.
1985 MEGA BLOKS	Ritvik Toy Corp.
1986 Magna Doodle	Fisher-Price, Div. of Mattel
1986 Encore	Endless Games
1986 Flannelboard Fun Kit	Roylco
1987 Pictionary	Hasbro, Inc.
1987 Jenga	Milton Bradley Co.
1987 Koosh Ball	OddzOn, Div. of Hasbro, Inc.
1988 Mutant Ninja Turtles	Playmates Toys, Inc.
1988 Micro Machines	Galoob Toys, Div. of Hasbro
1989 Super Soaker	Larami, Div. of Hasbro, Inc.
1989 So Soft Baby Doll	Learning Curve International

100 TOP TOYS OF THE CENTURY

The Toy Industry Association has named the top 100 toys of the last 100 years:

1900

Lionel Trains

1903

Crayola Crayons

1903

Flinch Card Game

1903

Ideal Commonwealth Teddy Bears

1906

Tootsietoy Model T Ford

1913

Erector Sets

1913

Tinkertoys

1915

Raggedy Ann

1916

Lincoln Logs

1917

Radio Flyer Wagon

1923

Madame Alexander Dolls

1929

Duncan Yo-Yo

1930

Mickey & Minnie Mouse

1932

Tripoley Game

1934

Sorry Game

1935

Monopoly

1937

Betsy Wetsy

1938

View-Master

1942

Nok-Hockey

1947

Tonka Trucks

1947

John Deere Die Cast

1947

Magic 8 Ball

1948

Cootie

1948

Scrabble

1948

Slinky

1949

Candy Land

1949

Clue

1950

Silly Putty

1951

Ginny Dolls

1952

Mr. Potato Head

1953

Colorforms

1953

LEGO Building Sets

1954

Matchbox Cars

1955

Wooly Willy

1956

Play-Doh

1956

Uncle Milton Original Ant Farm

1956

Yahtzee Game

1957

Corn Popper

1957

Frisbee

1958

Hula Hoop

1959

Barbie

1960

BRIO Wooden Toys

1960

Etch-A-Sketch

1960

Game of Life

1961

Slip N' Slide

1961

Troll Dolls

1962

Chatter Telephone

1963

Easy Bake Oven

1964

G.I.Joe

1965

Creepy Crawlers

1965

Operation Game

1965

See 'n' Say

1966

Twister Game

1967

Battleship Game

1967

Big Wheel

1967

Ker Plunk

1967

Lite Brite

1968

Hot Wheels

1970

Nerf Balls

1971

Mastermind

1972

Uno Card Game

1973

Shrinky Dinks

1974

Dungeons and Dragons Game

1974

Playmobil

1975

Ilo Game

1976

Magna Doodle

1977

Star Wars Action Figures

1978

Hungry Hungry Hippos

1978

Rubik's Cube

1978

Simon Electronic Game

1979

Cozy Coupe Ride-On

1979

Strawberry Shortcake

1982

Stompers

1982

Trivial Pursuit

1983

Cabbage Patch Kids

1983

Care Bears

1983

My Little Pony

1984

Transformers

1985

Scruples Game

1985

Teddy Ruxpin

1986

Pound Puppies

1987

Koosh Ball

1987

Pictionary Game

1988

Teenage Mutant Ninja Turtles

1989

Super Soaker

1992

Barney Plush

1992

K'NEX Building Sets

1993

Magic: The Gathering Card Game

1994

Mighty Morphin Power Rangers

1995

Lamaze Learning Products

1996

Beanie Babies

1996

Tickle-Me Elmo

1997

Bass Fishin' Game

1997

Tamagotchi

1998

Rescue Heroes

1998

Furby

1999

Groovy Girls

1999

Leap Frog Leap Pad

2000

Razor scooter

2000

Jumbo Music Block

THE TOY INDUSTRY HALL OF FAME

1985

HERMAN G. FISHER

Fisher-Price

JEROME M. FRYER

CBS Toys/Gabriel Industries

A.C. GILBERT, SR.

A.C. Gilbert Company

MARVIN GLASS

Marvin Glass & Associates

NATHAN GREENMAN

Greenman Brothers, Inc

MERRILL L. HASSENFELD

Hasbro, Inc.

LOUIS MARX

Louis Marx Toy Company

1986

GEORGE S. PARKER

Parker Brothers

CHARLES S. RAIZEN

Transogram

RAYMOND P. WAGNER

Mattel, Inc.

1987

JOSHUA LIONEL COWEN

Lionel Corporation

WALT DISNEY

Walt Disney Company

1988

WALTER W. ARMATYS

Toy Industry Association

MOREY W. KASCH

M.W. Kasch Company

JAMES J. SHEA, SR.

Milton Bradley Company

1989

OLE KIRK CHRISTIANSEN

LEGO Group

RUTH and ELLIOT HANDLER

Mattel, Inc.

BENJAMIN F. MICHTOM

Ideal Toy Corporation

1990

CHARLES LAZARUS

Toys 'R' Us

EDWARD P. PARKER

Parker Brothers

1991

HENRY COORDS

Fisher-Price

STEPHEN D. HASSENFELD

Hasbro, Inc.

1992

JIM HENSON

Jim Henson Productions, Inc.

BERNARD LOOMIS

Bernard Loomis, Inc.

1993

AARON LOCKER

Locker, Greenberg & Brainin

ALBERT STEINER

Kenner Products Company

1994

ALAN G. HASSENFELD

Hasbro, Inc.

1995

JOHN W. AMERMAN

Mattel, Inc.

1996

RICHARD E. GREY

Tyco Toys, Inc.

1997

THOMAS J. KALINSKE

Knowledge Universe, L.L.C.

HOWARD MOORE

Toys 'R' Us

SY ZIV

Sy Ziv Associates, Inc.

1998

JEFFREY BRESLOW

HOWARD MORRISON

ROUBEN TERZIAN

Breslow Morrison Terzian & Associates

RUSSELL L. WENKSTERN

Tonka Toys

1999

MICHAEL GOLDSTEIN

Toys 'R' Us

2000

BEATRICE ALEXANDER BEHRMAN

Alexander Doll Company, Inc.

FRED F. ERTL, JR.

Ertl Company, Inc.

2001
BETTY M. JAMES

James Industries Inc.

2002
DAVID A. MILLER

Toy Industry Association

2003
EDDY GOLDFARB

Eddy Goldfarb, Inc.

ANTONIO PASIN

Radio Flyer

2004
MILTON BRADLEY

Hasbro Games

GEORGE DITOMASSI

Hasbro International

NEIL B. FRIEDMAN

Fisher-Price Brands of Mattel

2005

REUBEN KLAMER

Reuben Klamer Toylab

LIONEL WEINTRAUB

Ideal Toy Corporation

GUIDE TO TOY MANUFACTURERS
FEATURED IN
THE RIGHT TOYS

Alex Toys
800-666-2539
www.alextoys.com

American Girl/Pleasant Company
800-845-0005
www.americangirl.com

ATOLLO Global Ltd/ATOLLO
866-428-6556
www.atollo.com

AURORA
888-287-6722
www.auroragift.com

Baby Einstein Company
800-793-1454
www.babyeinstein.com

BATTAT Incorporated
800-822-8828
www.battat-toys.com

Binary Arts
703-549-4999
www.binaryarts.com

Birdcage Books
866-424-1701
www.birdcagebooks.com

Briarpatch
800-232-7427
www.briarpatch.com

BRIO Corporation
888-274-6869
www.brio.net

Chicco USA, Inc.
877-424-4226
www.chiccousa.com

Colorforms (University Games)
415-503-1600
www.ugames.com

Corolle
800-628-3655
www.corolledolls.com

Cranium, Inc.
877-CRANIUM
www.cranium.com

Crayola Products (Binney & Smith)
800-CRAYOLA
www.crayola.com

Creativity for Kids
800-311-8684 x3037
www.creativityforkids.com

Curiosity Kits, Inc.
800-584-5487
www.curiositykits.com

Design Science Toys
800-227-2316
www.dstoys.com

Educational Insights/GeoSafari
800-995-4436
www.educationalinsights.com

Faber-Castell USA / Creativity for Kids
800-311-8684 ext. 3037
www.creativityforkids.com

The First Years
800-225- 0382
www.thefirstyears.com

Fisher-Price
800-432-KIDS
www.fisherprice.com

Folkmanis, Inc.
800-654-8922
www.folkmanis.com

Front Porch Classics / Old Century Classics
206-826-3202
www.frontporchclassics.com

Funrise Toy Corporation
800-882-3808
www.funrise.com

Games For All Reasons
781-648-2029
www.game-board.com

Gotz Dolls, Inc.
800-959-3655
www.gotzdolls.com

Guidecraft USA
800-544-6526
www.guidecraft.com

Gund
800-448-GUND
www.gund.com

Haba (TC Timber/Habermaass)
800-468-6873
www.habausa.com

Hasbro, Inc.
(Playskool) 800-752-9755
(Milton Bradley) 888-836-7025
www.hasbro.com

Hoberman Designs
888-229-3653
www.hoberman.com

Insect Lore
800-LIVE BUG
www.insectlore.com

International Playthings
800-445-8347
www.intplay.com

Kid Galaxy, Inc. / My First RC
800-816-1135
www.kidgalaxy.com

Klutz
800-737-4123
www.klutz.com

K'NEX Industries
800-822-5639
www.knex.com

Lauri Toys
800-451-0520

Leapfrog Enterprises, Inc.
800-701-LEAP
www.leapfrog.com

Learning Curve International
(Eden)
(Lamaze)
800-704-8697
www.learningcurve.com

Learning Resources, Inc.
888-800-7893
www.learningresources.com

LEGO
800-453-4652
www.lego.com

Lights, Camera, Interaction
203-846-8046

Lillian Vernon/Lilly's Kids
800-545-5426
www.lillianvernon.com

Link Innovations
978-276-0424
www.constructionjack.com

Little Tikes
800-321-0183
www.littletikes.com

Magnetic Poetry, Inc.
800-370-7697
www.magneticpoetry.com

Malibu Toys
818-360-7521
www.malibutoys.com

Manhattan Toy
800-541-1345
www.manhattantoy.com

Maple Landmark
800-421-4223
www.maplelandmark.com

Mary Meyer Corporation
800-451-438
www.marymeyer.com

Mattel, Inc.
800-524-8697
www.mattel.com

Mega Bloks, Inc.
800-465-6342
www.megabloks.com

Miggle Toys, Inc.
877-432-0140
www.miggle.com

Munchkin, Inc.
800-344-2229
www.munchkininc.com

Neurosmith
800-220-3669
www.neurosmith.com

North American Bear Co / Build-a-Clown Stacking Toy
800-682-3427
www.nabear.com

The Ohio Art Company
800-800-3141
www.world-of-toys.com

OOZ & OZ
www.oozandoz.com

Orion Telescopes & Binoculars
800-447-1001
www.telescope.com

Outset Media Corp
877-592-7374
www.outsetmedia.com

Peg Perego USA
800-728-2108
www.perego.com

Playmobil
800-PLAYMOBIL
www.playmobil.com

Radio Flyer
800-621-7613
www.radioflyer.com

Razor USA
888-467-2967
www.razorusa.com

RC2 Corporation / Ertl
888-281-1824
www.rcertl.com

Rokenbok
888-476-5265
www.rokenbok.com

Sassy
800-323-6336
www.sassybaby.com

Schylling
800-767-8697
www.schylling.com

Scientific Explorer
800-900-1182
www.scientificexplorer.com

Shelcore
732-764-9000
www.shelcore.com

Silver Dolphin Books
800-284-3580
www.silverdolphinbooks.com

The Singing Machine Co., Inc.
954-596-1000
www.singingmachine.com

Small World Toys/Ryan's Room
800-310-1717
www.smallworldtoys.com

Spin Master Ltd.
800-622-8339
www.spinmaster.com

Sport-Fun
800-423-2597
www.sportfun.com

Spring International, Inc. / Dig It Up! - NY
888-238-8303
www.digitup-NY.com

Think Fun
800-468-1864
www.ThinkFun.com

Today's Plastics / Today's Kids
800-258-8697
www.todayskids.com

TOMY
949-955-1030
www.tomy.com

Uncle JimStones
800-830-2191
www.unclejimstones.com

Uncle Milton
818-707-0224
www.unclemilton.com

VTech Electronics North America
800-521-2010
www.vtechkids.com

Wild Planet Toys / Room Gear
800-247-6570
www.roomgear.com

Woodkins by Pamela Drake Inc.
800-966-3762
www.woodkins.com

Zapf Creation
877-629-9273
www.zapf-creation.com

About The Author

Dr. Helen Boehm

Dr. Helen Boehm is a distinguished psychologist and nationally known authority on children's development, play and media. She is a trusted parenting resource and frequent guest on television.

A longtime advocate for responsible children's media, Dr. Boehm headed Public Responsibility and Network Standards at MTV Networks/ Nickelodeon and was Vice President of the Fox Children's Network. She has given testimony on TV programming and advertising before the U.S. Congress and is the mother of two children.

LaVergne, TN USA
05 November 2009
163141LV00003B/148/A